AFTERTHOUGHTS
An Anthology of Rhode Island Veterans

Edited by
Amber Bliss & Sara Deignan

Cover Art and Design by
Rashaa Al-Sasah

2024

AFTERTHOUGHTS
An Anthology of Rhode Island Veterans
Edited by Amber Bliss & Sara Deignan

West Warwick Public Library
1043 Main Street
West Warwick, RI 02893
www.wwpl.org

This project was made possible in part by a grant from the Rhode Island State Council on the Arts, through an appropriation by the Rhode Island General Assembly and a grant from the National Endowment for the Arts.

Acknowledgements

We want to thank our friends at the Rhode Island State Council on the Arts for their generous funding as well as their support of writing, including genre writing, as art, which is rarer than you'd think. A special thanks to Kimberly Ferrante at the Providence VA Medical Center for her guidance, support, and commitment to the success of this project. We'd be remiss if we didn't thank our colleague and co-director of the press, Rashaa Al-Sasah, who works behind the scenes on most of these publications in the trenches of administration, problem solving, and design. A special thanks to Kristen Bezner, who shoulders the herculean task of copyediting while simultaneously managing all of the technology in the library. A special thank you to Julianna Risica, who offered her expertise in poetry and constructed and taught our first poetry module alongside Kristen. Finally, a huge thank you to all of the staff at the West Warwick Public Library who proofread and copyedited until their vision was blurry, as well as endlessly stepped up to cover desks and other tasks throughout the library while my attention was diverted on this project. These projects could not be done without you.

Contents

Introduction

Afterthoughts is an anthology of Rhode Island Veterans, but it is not about war. Many of our writers have been to war, they've certainly all been touched by it, but what *Afterthoughts* is really about is all of the spaces before, between, and after war.

Going into this anthology we expected to see courage in the form of service, of bravery in action, of all the things that first come to mind when you think of soldiers and the military—but our authors surprised us by showing us so much more. This is a deeply personal collection where the authors in these pages share not only the struggles and difficulties associated with service, but also the triumphs, joys, and relationships formed because of, or in spite of, their service.

When this project first started and everyone came together in our first Zoom class, all the writers had two things in common: their military service and their passion for the arts. Our writers are not just soldiers, not just plastic G.I. Joes, but nuanced, dynamic human beings who bonded over their passions for surfcasting, photography, cinema, and science fiction—to name a few. They're artists. Each of them answered a call to service that demanded hard things, sometimes destructive things, but in their personal lives they've all chosen to create.

And what a collection of creations they are. Our writers have shared poetry, flash fiction, and horror, as well as humor, sci-fi, and epistolary work. We even have an epic in verse. We hope that in spending time with these works, you will get a sense of the people behind them, of the relationships they cherish, the laughs they've shared, and their commitment to serving their communities and each other long after their required duties have ended.

~AMBER BLISS &
SARA DEIGNAN
June 2024

Twelve (Letters Home)

by
Tom Morrissey

November 14, 1969

Hi Mom and Dad,

Well, just a couple more weeks until I finish flight school. In a way I can't wait, but in even more ways I kinda wish I could just stay here, a cadet forever. Life is planned out every day. No decisions (ha ha). Just get up, make your bed, eat, clean the latrine, and go flying. You don't even have to decide on what to wear. I guess I'm becoming the son you wanted when it comes to the "make the bed every morning" part of it. Anyway, things are moving along fast and I'm sorry for not writing again in so long. Funny, every week we seem to be treated better, more politely. With respect, even from the sergeants that teach us in class. Just a few weeks ago they called us maggots and slime-balls.

Getting close to the big promotion to Warrant Officer WO1, getting those bars and wings, and then they will have to call us sir. Some already do. Can't wait to be coming home for a couple weeks before shipping out. Ft. Dix and then flying the rest of the way we hope. Some guys go on boats… sucks! Now here's a thought! A few of us who live close to the City might carpool and make one big road trip out of reporting. Party, party, party in the Big Apple.

There is a lot of paperwork we have to fill out almost every day. It's all a bit of a joke. I put you both down as beneficiaries on my $10,000 insurance policy, and you'll get my Mach I too, fully paid for. Something else you can fight over. But, I kind of hope you don't get either. I wanted you to know anyway. They sell us special insurance here that will pay it off, even if I died by "an act of war." Pretty good deal. Some of the guys are talking about buying Corvettes or XKEs to get the most for their money. Me, I like my Mustang. I hope you two are getting along better.

We had to fill out Duty Assignment Request forms. There's another one for ya. We were told to fill in Vietnam as our first choice and it really didn't matter what the other two were. That's how they can keep telling people that everyone there has volunteered to go. I decided I would totally miss the target when we qualified with the M-16, thinking I wouldn't qualify to get sent to Nam. So I put it on full automatic and shot 30 rounds in about five seconds!

I got sharpshooter. Can't say I didn't try to get stuck in the States!

Sorry to report, but letters I get aren't as frequent as they used to be when I first went in. And I'm no better! Sorry. Writing feels so meaningless after a while. Wish we could talk more. Oh well. Jenny used to write almost every day when I was in Basic. So did some of the guys and Uncle Bill. But I guess a year and a half wears on folks and gets redundant. I mean, how many times can someone ask you how you are or tell you about their lawn, school, or their job? Even Jimbo hasn't written in a while. He got himself involved with some sorta SDS or something at WJC. Not sure what SDS is. Have you heard of it?

In other news, my new favorite song is by a guy called Country Joe. He's a vet. It's called I-Feel-Like-I'm-Fixin'-to-Die Rag. It came out about a year ago, but seems more personal to me now. He sang it at Woodstock. Now there's a contrast. Mike, Jeff, Sara, Michelle, and Jenny all went in Jimbo's piece of crap van. Glad it wasn't that far of a drive. She told me not to be jealous, but I can't help it. Promised me that she wasn't one of the people running around in the mud naked. Guess I'll find out when I get home, hopefully in time for Thanksgiving. I'll have my orders by then, too. Probably leave for Nam around Christmas. Bummer!

I know you want to know more about what's happening here. We are flying more and sitting in classrooms less. One of my buddies had a chip-detector light come on the other day. It means the transmission may be falling apart. Scared him shitless (oops, sorry). Nothing happened though and the instructors all gave him high-fives for keeping his cool. Not like you can just pull into the breakdown lane.

"Just a drill," they said, "just wait!" Ha, "can't wait" is more like it. Finally get to use this stuff that's been packed into my brain for the last year and a half for real.

We still hear a lot about Tet last year. Still making the news on TV too. My current IP for tactics was there. Every day I learn some new flying-survival skill that's not exactly by the book. Glad he is my instructor. He promised me he would show up at graduation and have a drink with me as none of you can make the trip. Too bad, maybe someday I can show you around "Mother Rucker" as we call it.

Well, I need to go for now. We are going for advanced tactics this week and will be bivouacked somewhere with a creek for water. We're told it's more comfortable to sleep in the Huey on the steel floor than on the ground. Probably is. Quicker response time, too, when the rockets and mortars come in. Looking for a real adventure. I'll write more when I get back. See you soon.

Love, JR.

PS: Haven't seen Lance since we left Walters. He went to Hunter Stewart in GA for fixed wing transition. Seems his uncle made good on his promise. He'll be safe as hell and first in line for an airline job flying 727s in a year for sure.

January 11, 1970

Hello everyone,

Sorry I haven't written in so long. Finally started to get settled yesterday! And yes, I'm still alive. It took forever to get assigned to a unit, get issued all my equipment including a trenching tool and my .45, 1911 handgun. I hope I don't ever have to use either! A bunch of other stuff too, like a canteen, poncho, etc. But I now have a bed in a "hootch."

So, about the last couple of weeks, it feels like I'm on a totally different planet. The flights here were miserable. We stopped everywhere it seems. Traveled some in a cargo plane with canvas-meshed seats along the wall facing the center. No windows. Not a typical passenger jet like at the airport. We were shuffled here and there, loaded and reloaded. Didn't see my duffle bag for a couple of days either, which made me a bit worried. Even stayed overnight in Guam and saw Mt. Fuji from the plane window on New Year's Eve.

I'm assigned to the 117th Assault Helicopter Company near Long Binh. But you don't put this in my address when you write me. My mailing address is my name, 117th AHC, APO 71891-7261, San Francisco. I'll get it. I guess part of military security is not putting addresses on envelopes. Although it is sort of stupid as we have all kinds of Vietnamese working on base and they all know who we are and what unit we are in and all of that. "Military Intelligence." An oxymoron for sure. And did you notice, we get to just write "free" on the envelope and no stamp. If you noticed, I added "dom" to it. "FREEdom."

So, I was unable to really write much of anything other than that postcard of Mt. Fuji. Pretty cool! I never unpacked until now. Got assigned to a "replacement battalion" and sat there for a couple days, then rode around in the back of deuce-and-a-half trucks, dropped off at one place, then another. Finally, me and another guy, Lee, got picked up at a helipad and flown around for about half a day until we landed at some fire support base. Middle of nowhere. We were both afraid that we were getting stationed there. But, thank God, the next morning another chopper came and picked us up for the hour-long ride to Plantation Airfield. Saw a lot of the country from the air. That chopper was from our new unit and had a Pink Panther on the nose cone. Home sweet home at last. I'll send you some pictures as soon as I get a camera. A Nikon. I want a Nikon!

The hootch I am living in is really a tent with wooden floors. Everyone sort of clears out a spot for themselves and has a foot locker, a cot, and a thin mattress. I took over a spot from a guy who made his DEROS and went home uninjured. Thank God for small favors. Mattresses are not taken for granted here. The tent leaks, so the poncho will pay for itself. I have it strung over my cot to keep me dry. We had a bit of a shower yesterday and it's not even rainy season yet so I hate to think how bad it will be when the monsoons get here in a few months. The guys in my platoon (Second Platoon) are nice but try to come across as hard-asses. They call us "newbies." One guy, Deedy, has a chicken plate (chest protector) with a .51 Cal round stuck in it. He had it under his seat which is where most guys use it. I like him. He's from Boston. (Lee is in the First Platoon.)

I already had my first checkride and it was adventurous. They don't waste any time here once you get placed. I was up flying and doing autorotations before I even got the sheets on my bed. We have a makeshift O-Club with a Vietnamese barmaid. If you put your hat on the bar, you have to buy everyone there a round. And, you can't wear it inside, but you have to wear it outside at all times. I hate hats! What a pain.

During my checkride, a mortar hit the revetment area and my IP just pulled pitch. We were 100 feet in the air before you could say "boo!" We flew out into some hills nearby looking for Charlie, you know, the VC, Viet Cong, but, thankfully, didn't see any. It was just him and me in the helicopter with no crew or guns.

The first thing I did when I got here and had a few hours free was to walk to the post exchange (PX) about a mile away. Actually, you hitchhike and inevitably someone passing in a fuel truck or something stops and gives you a lift. That's where I got this cool stationery to write this letter on. I'm also writing to Jenny. I hope she is good. It was so nice being with her and everyone last month. Especially having Christmas together with you and Dad. In fact, I'm using that nice pen you guys gave me to write this very letter. Practical gift if there ever was one!

Well, so long for now. I'll try to write often but I have no idea what to expect. Sometimes, guys from our unit are gone for several days in the field. As an aviation unit we have no grunts, so we get farmed out to LRRPs, Special Forces (Green Berets), Navy SEALs, or sometimes to what we call "Ruff Puffs"—Vietnamese forces. Mean guys, on missions we are not supposed to write about.

Anyway, the mess hall is open and I'm going to go eat. Food is ok and, what a rip off, officers have to pay for our meals. Most of us just walk the mile to the O-Club. As long as we have to pay for it anyway, might as well have a steak.

Love.

JR

PS: Everything here smells really bad. They burn the shit (sorry) from the toilets in 55-gallon barrels every day behind the latrines using JP4, jet fuel. Good in my Zippo lighter too! Billowing smelly, black smoke. And it is hot as hell 24/7. With the humidity and dust, it is literally steamy and dirty air outside and inside. No air conditioning. Makes being in the air a blessing.

Just ate and found out I'm going on my first mission tomorrow. More later.

March 21, 1970

Hi Dad,

Mom told me Lance got killed. I got her letter yesterday. One from Lance too. Read his first. We were planning to meet up soon. He flies Otters and flies down here often picking up shit. He sent me his unit frequency. It's screwed up, getting both of them the same day. I felt numb. Went to the club and had a steak and a million scotches. "Happy Hour," as his mom would say.

Mom also said you moved out. I'm sorry to hear. I know you guys have your differences but, hell dad, this is MY family too isn't it? Don't I have a say in this? I mean I'm here getting frigging shot at every day, fighting for survival here. And you two can't figure simple shit like getting along and following orders? Yeah, I said that. "Following orders!" Having the gumption to stick to your commitments, your vows. Now here I go sounding like a Catholic again and you know me, I'm not any Catholic and surely no Catholic's son. Sure, we went to Mass and I got sent to Catholic School too, but I learned from the best as you always said. Crap, I mean if I decided to abandon a mission, like the ones we have been on lately, I'd be court-martialed or shot. Is asking you two to work this out too much? I really don't think so. And don't worry, I'm telling her the same thing too.

JR

PS.

I'm fine and sorry to dump on you so much. It's just that Jenny and now this, I really am wondering what the fuck I'm fighting for. Why do we want to survive at all if this shit is all that we get when it's all said and done. At least we have the O-Club to go to, and that's where I'm heading now.

April 14, 1970

Hi Mom and Dad,

Well, like I said, this is bull writing two letters, so you two both can share one. Shit hit the fan here last week. We're really not supposed to write this stuff in a letter as it is "confidential," but it's in the news everywhere, even here and on Gook TV. We had a big "secret" mission into Cambodia the other day. Very like James Bond. No markings on the aircraft and we were even given flight suits with no name tags or insignias on them. I told you we were working with the Special Forces, SEALS and MACVSOG with training Cambodians. Well, we dumped a bunch of these Cambodian Khmer mercenaries in, way across the border. At least 20 klicks. We took a few rounds and I about shit my pants. Got my cherry popped as they say. A real crappy sound, rounds hitting the ship. Several got shot down, in flames sometimes. None from our unit. Really spooky flying back across the fence looking down on them, all burnt up and such. They looked sorta like huge stingrays laying in the sand under the water. Silent and spooky.

TWELVE (LETTERS HOME)

Anyway, enough of that. I know you want to know stuff but there is too much stuff and it would take all day. And, in the end it would just worry you guys and you have enough on your plates as it is. But I need to talk to someone sometimes who's not here in it.

You said you saw Jenny at Sears the other day. I really don't want to even hear her name. She sent me that proverbial "Dear John" letter last week. She's attending WJC and hanging out with Jimbo and those SDS folks I wrote about earlier. Seems they see themselves as "better people" for not going to Vietnam. In a way I understand it. The place here is a total mess and probably should just be mowed down and repaved. At least that's the sentiment here. But we shall see how Jimbo's draft number works out! Joke may be on him!

Everyone here is corrupt. Especially the Vietnamese politicians. LBJ and Lady Bird are the worst though. Seems they own almost every company that does business over here. Some scandal with Carling Black Label beer too. Seems some sergeant is making millions stocking it over here. I still stick to scotch though. Just like I was taught! Ha Ha. So, maybe Nixon still might win this thing if they would let us. I don't think he makes as much from the war as LBJ did. But who knows.

Speaking of corrupt. We get paid here in MPC (Military Payment Certificates) so there won't be any US Currency floating around. But it's worth double on the black market in Saigon. So, if you will, go to the bank and send me a couple hundred in $20 bills in your next letter. This BS about them reading our mail is not true. I don't know of anyone who has gotten caught. I can exchange it for Vietnamese money or MPC here for a big profit. Then go shopping.

I look forward to hearing from you and glad to know that the weather has warmed up there. Have you planted any tomatoes yet?

More later

JR

PS: I am putting in for my R&R. Takes a couple months to process. Hope to go to Australia but Japan is my second choice. I'll let you know. Don't forget the $$$!

TWELVE (LETTERS HOME)

May 29, 1970

Hi Mom and Dad,

Thanks for your cards,, the western belt, and the genuine handmade "leathery" sandals. Especially the sandals. I got them last week. Wore them to the Club that very night. They fit perfectly. Way better than the ones they make here like the VC wear. Bet you used my old pair to get the size right. Thank Charlie for me! My birthday was great, considering. The pilots in my platoon have a tradition when it comes to birthdays, but I'll just leave it at that. Thanks again!

Lot's happened since my last letter. I'm sure I told you about being picked to start learning to transition to the left seat. Well I did it, passed the checkrides, and actually flew a couple of missions already as AC (Aircraft Commander. Very cool. I have my own call sign now, Warlord 23. Pretty cool, it's a prime number. See, I learned something in those math classes. This is what a call sign means: My unit is the Warlords and I'm in the Second Platoon so the 2. The 3 is not significant at the platoon level. It was just the only number not being used currently as McEntire (Mac) who was Warlord 23 made his DEROS date unscathed. Hope that's a good sign and a lucky number too. The hootch maids giggle at me because for the Chinese the number 23 means "someone of great popular charm." Psychedelic "druggies" here are called "heads." We have a few in our unit. One everyone calls "Moon Man." He said 23 stands for an enigma. So it could go either way. We'll see in a few more months won't we.

They say that in flight school we learned to fly the helicopter but here, we learn to use it! It's amazing, the aircraft almost feels like an extension of my body. It is really becoming a part of me. I can almost just think it to do something and it does. Control movements are so subtle. It's almost like having a cat on your lap and stroking it. I mean the slightest touch. Hard to explain. But cool as hell.

In my last couple of letters I've been telling you about shit going on here. I am glad you told me not to worry about clearing off my chest and telling you. I don't want to make you worry but at the same time, I know that if I didn't tell you anything your minds would run wild with worry. Especially with the daily reporting they have on TV from here. It's not like you Dad, in WW2 with just the glorified highlights of giant battles. This place is shitty; hand-to-hand combat for the guys in the boonies, and we bring them in and out, too often in body bags. At the risk of being too gross, sometimes they aren't even in body bags, maybe still alive and blown to shit. We take them to a field hospital and fly around all day with bloody skin and guts splattered around the ship. When we pull up to POL, we need to hose her down and scrub the floors. Glad it's the crew's responsibility and not me who gets stuck with that.

Speaking of scrubbing the floors, we had to fly a gook prisoner to Cu Chi a couple days ago. He was blindfolded with hands and feet tied tight. Anyway, he was sitting there in the cargo bay with no doors, bouncing around with wind blowing in his face. Must have felt strange. The guy had probably never been in a plane, much less a helicopter before. I snapped a great shot of him in the bay. Can't wait to see it. So, we made a couple of sharp turns. Really sharp-banked turns evading some fire. The kind of turns that make you want to hold on to something. I think he must have thought we were getting ready to toss him out. He looked scared shitless, and I guess actually was. He shit his pants. What a mess. Worst crap smell ever! It's their diet! But don't worry, I would never just throw someone out of the aircraft in mid-air. I still have some upbringing left.

I got this really cool SKS Russian rifle another day in a big cache we captured at a place about 40 klicks northeast of Tay Ninh. Just occurred to me… that's a birthday present too, from Chuck. Tay Ninh is where that big mountain, Núi Bà Đen is. They have some cool shit there. There's a big church, the Cao Tai temple. They worship everyone, even Charlie Chaplin. True! And the mountain is allegedly occupied by the "Black Virgin," a legendary goddess who gets a big pilgrimage every year that just happened a couple weeks ago. Another bullshit opportunity for a ceasefire during which we allow Charlie to rearm. At least I got one of their guns out of the deal.

I took a picture of me and my ship on the top but it's a color slide so you won't be able to see it until I get home. Anyway, you probably know more about the official story of what's going on here from the news and Walter Cronkite than I do. We were supporting the 25th Infantry and the Cav guys. We sometimes fly C&C with the generals watching the war from 1,500 feet, but we still get into the shit enough to need a shower at the end of the day (joke!). We let down and insert guys here or there as the battle unfolds, holding at a hover while the ship's weight shifts, maybe the tip of one skid touching the ground or a big rock. Dodging branches. Haul wounded if a medevac isn't handy. I still can't believe those guys are unarmed. When they send us, we shoot back! Last week, we had a few Donut Dollies and a stack of body bags in the ship at the same time. Sucks.

In other news, we had another big steak fry. They are grilled so I'll never understand why they call it a "steak fry." Anyway, I had a free day so the CO conscripted me and a wad of cash in Vietnamese money, a 3/4-ton truck and driver (with a gunner), and we took off to "downtown" (if you can call it that) Long Bing to a bakery and butcher shop. I guess these places contract a lot with the military. I have never seen so much raw meat or fresh hot bread at once in my life. What a trip. We had the vehicle for as long as we needed it, and we took our time. A couple of other guys snuck on with us and spent their day getting drunk and stoned, skipping from titty-bar to titty-bar trying to bang as many short-time girls as they could. I guess this sorta grosses you out Mom, but this place is not where you raised me to be. "Fucken this or that" comes out of my mouth in every sentence along with "shit," the most flexible words in the English language. Between that, the strippers, the barmaids, beer and Saigon Tea, (oh yeah, and killing people every day!), then drinking and listening to the Moody Blues or something singing about peace and love… I'm turning into something. We all are… what, I don't know.

Dad, someday we'll have to compare notes. I'm curious just how similar or different my combat experience is from yours.

My R&R was approved for Australia. Should be early next month. Guess I'm going with the Minolta. No Nikon yet! Still on order, can't wait.

Gotta eat and get some sleep as tomorrow is gonna be the first of many long ones.

Love JR

TWELVE (LETTERS HOME)

June 29, 1970

Well, from the postcards I sent you, I bet you figured out that I had a great time on R&R. What a hoot! Nobody on the flight gave a damn, not even the couple of bird colonels. Free for all. As it turns out, I got my new Nikon just before leaving and was testing it out there. You're going to have to wait until I get home to see any more of my photos because I am trying to be "professional" and shoot color slides or an occasional roll of black and white which I can develop myself at the USO darkroom at Bien Hoa. I'm getting better with the black and white but I'll never forgive myself for fucking up the first couple of rolls as they had some pretty cool stuff on them. Once I get the R&R shots developed, I can send you some of the more wholesome ones.

Anyway, being able to call you guys on the phone from Sydney was the high point of the trip. (That and not getting rocketed or shot at for a week.) But it was so surreal being there, people driving around in cars (all small cars too) and doing normal stuff like going shopping or to the movies with their girl. The small stuff you don't even know you have until you're watching your friends get blown away instead. Oh well.

When we landed in Sydney they wouldn't let us off the plane right away. So then, after this guy comes on the plane and gives the speech on how to treat Aussies with respect and other bullshit, they shut the doors of the plane again and fumigated us. The whole inside of the plane. Then they made everyone (even the full birds) take off their shoes and inspected them, looking for any drugs people may have snuck in them. Lots of folks in Nam are doing smack, as I told you. Guess they can't just go cold turkey for a week to go see some round-eyes. Anyway, we finally got off that friggin' plane and were bussed to our hotels. It wasn't as nice as the pictures I saw in the brochure but it sure beat the cot I have in Nam. We all immediately went bar hopping and stayed out until daylight. Aussie guys like their beer, and the chicks seem unattended and were checking us out. I guess we are like the new models replacing last week's assortment that already got shipped back. Anyway, met a couple nice ladies and hung out with them for the next few days. Wow, money goes fast.

TWELVE (LETTERS HOME)

So, while I was on R&R, a ship from First Platoon was transporting a bunch of guys to Tan Son Nhut in Saigon, MACV Pad. What we call a "milk run." A couple of guys going on R&R and the XO on company business at MACV. Anyway, just after everyone got off, the ship exploded on take off, spun out of control and burned up right in front of everybody's eyes. The whole crew. One of the pilots, George, was set to go home next week and was essentially all packed and just waiting for his orders. He had no business being out there. Fuck. Friggin' CO. How fucked up can it get? How spooked everyone here has been. Especially the guys who had just gotten off, watching it all. Hell, I could have easily been on that flight too. The hootch maids wanted to have his radio. Fuck it, let 'em have it, I say. Not even a combat mission.

In other news, I've been offered the opportunity to take over the FireFly mission our unit has. It's flying at night, mostly in Cambodia. You get to sleep all day. Our sister unit, the "dollar ninety-five" we call it (the 195th AHC) is standing down and splitting up. And it comes with the opportunity for me to grab a hootch with an air conditioner. Sleep all day in cool AC!

Far-fucking-out! Anyway, I was toying with the mission before R&R as peter-pilot and I guess I did alright. It's a tight crew and they always fly together. Sorta like a family. Anyway, I'll let you know what happens. The ship is named Miss Hap, with Annie Fanny on the nose. Great play on words!

Well there is a gook band at the club tonight with two strippers. I know you cringe at this thought. Your Boy Scout and former altar boy, living this lifestyle, but what can I say? I'm in Rome and being Roman, I guess. So, that's that for now.

Love you both.

TWELVE (LETTERS HOME)

27 Aug, 1970

I don't normally get superstitious but things are weird sometimes. I finally started my short-timer's calendar last week. Everyone has one. Counting how many days until one's tour of duty in this shit-hole comes to an end. On that Freedom Bird, wheels up. Can't wait. Although there is a side of me that will miss the place, the rush and just the pure hell of it. Flying nights is a trip. I love it. We are free, just my ship and a gun ship, sometimes two depending on how much shit is expected to hit the fan on any given night. I don't think I explained the deal to you well enough before. So, to answer your questions, yes and no.

We essentially have two crews that take turns flying this mission as best we can. I pretty much do it every other night but sometimes 2-3 nights in a row. Depends. There are a couple of fill-in guys in case someone is sick. But as AC, I am not authorized to be sick. There is usually a line of guys wanting to go for the ride and extra guns come in handy sometimes but we have to be aware of the weight element. So, space is limited if you are interested in coming along!

The mission flies every night, weather permitting. We low-level up and down canals and "roads" looking for Charlie. If we find him, we light him up with our flood lights, .50 cal, and our minigun. The guns roll in behind us then the artillery. Clean and simple. But the night air. Being pretty much the only aircraft in the air in the whole country. How cool is that, especially for a kid right out of high school?

We navigate off of the AFVN Radio Tower near Saigon. It gives a fixed bearing home and some great tunes too. The night disc jockey is very hip and plays a mix of rock and jazz. We sometimes fly down to Dong Tam, a Navy base south of Saigon and there is a cook there who makes bagels every night. Imagine that. With cream cheese and everything. Even lox. We'll help the SEALs if they are in some shit too. Want a fun night? Try landing on a drifting PBR in the rain, in the dark without sinking it. Fair trade for a fresh bagel. But usually, we head northwest from Cu Chi up what is called Highway 13 into Cambodian airspace. Try not to take the same path every night. Mix it up a little. The border is very obvious with bomb craters walked right up to it on the Vietnamese side, so you really know when you cross over. And when we cross back over we all give a sigh of relief. Funny about that, feeling safer in VN.

I'm up for a DFC too because of a rescue mission at about 0200 (2 AM for you guys) a couple of nights ago. We were called to provide illumination and cover for a night medevac at some messed up fire support base in Bum-Fuck, Somewhere, South Vietnam. A set of coordinates, middle of nowhere. You gotta understand just how frigging dark it is here. No small towns, no street lights, nothing. Just black. They're being rocketed and under attack with small arms fire. We hauled ass there and the VC hightailed it when we pulled up. It was a piece of work watching the medevac ship come in below us in the total darkness, no lights. None of us have nav lights on at night. Don't want to give Charlie a better target than we already are. Afterwards, we combed the area shooting up every tree and bush we could find. We found an old guy crouched next to a rice paddy dike. He put his hands up. I would too if I was in his position. Three US Army helos circled around him. We captured him and brought him to Cu Chi TOC where he was interrogated. We just refueled and went back to work. Rest of the night was dull by contrast and we just bored holes in the sky pretty much until our station time was used up.

OK, enough war stories. I'm sorta freaked about counting down my remaining days. 135 and a wake up! Too confident? Maybe so. Getting so short I can hardly see above the table! But thinking about extending too. Maybe fly Cobras or VIP in 58s. At least I wouldn't have being short to worry about anymore!

Love ya,

JR

TWELVE (LETTERS HOME)

September 8, 1970

Boring!

Well it's monsoon season here in III Corps and it rains pretty much every minute. And if it's not raining, the cloud cover and visibility is too low to really fly much more than some emergency resupply missions and evacuations. Nights are even worse. We sit and wait on standby most of the time. Had to put it near Cu Chi the other night due to weather closing in. Felt a bit uneasy doing it. Not exactly an airport. Lots of coffee to say the least.

Nothing to really report. Usually we are sitting around in the flight ops room, several of us are finally getting an opportunity to get to know each other beyond our call signs and flying abilities. Funny to think, but we all had lives and aspirations before Nam. I hope I can resume mine. The idea of an airline job still looms over my head when I lay in bed trying to get to sleep. I hope there's one waiting for me when I get back. When the weather breaks, we do go out. Like I said, had to land at some unsavory places a few times as the rains picked back up and the clouds got too low. We'll fly in just about anything if it means saving some GIs in the shit. But that's about it.

I made the mistake of thinking I could fly on instruments in the rain the other night. Would have worked out better if I knew where the heck I was. I managed to keep straight and level on a heading. Clouds broke and suddenly there were trees in front of me as we approached the side of a mountain at 80 knots. Good thing for a bright moon that night. They call that a "cumulo-granite" rather than a cumulonimbus cloud. A bit of combat humor to throw at you.

In my final report of the evening (actually morning!) before hitting the sack, I have an even newer favorite song. Everybody here loves it, although it's pretty much an in-joke among us so you may not be able to appreciate it. Try flying combat missions while listening to The Temptations new hit "War" as you engage with both barrels. I'm sure you've heard it, just not in this context. This reminds me, Jimbo finally made contact. He sent me a clipping from the paper showing them all at an antiwar rally at WJC holding a sign that said "Baby

Killers." I'm sure you saw that in the paper too. Thanks for not sending it.

9 September, '70

Dad,

I think I'm starting to understand you better. I know I said I was going to write both you and Mom in one letter, but I guess I lied. I feel I see you better now as a person rather than that guy always on my case about some shit thing or the other. I've been issued a pair of Bullshit Detectors. Like you said, I wear them daily. I can see more clearly.

Flew a screwy mission yesterday. Poked around very low level with some guys from MACV Headquarters adding up a body count out in some rice paddies west of here. (We drop the SOG part as a rule) Weird. So peaceful. No clouds, sunny. Nice music in my ears and these guys counting dead dinks in the shallow water. Good thing I had my Bullshit Detectors with me. Ha!

Just being here, wondering what the hell it's all about. Must have been the same for you, too. I know, yours was "the big one." We hear that shit all the time. But it's only as big as what immediately surrounds you. All war is local isn't it?

I mean, I now see you as a fellow soldier even more so than my dad. I mean, you're both. Don't get me wrong. But you are far more than I ever gave you credit for. Even Mom, I don't think she fully gets it, really. I mean, sure, she cares, but there is a line she can't cross. I've seen it now and I don't think she, Jimbo, the other assholes back home… Jenny, the antiwar protesters… any of them get it. What the fuck do they know! Nothing, like that song says: "War, what is it good for? Nothing."

But I think he is wrong. Yeah the guy who wrote it, I heard, is a vet. But not a combat vet. A REMF. Not like us. I think that's where the line gets drawn. We, you and me, we share that. Makes me sorta love you more. Maybe love you again. I think I get it.

Sorry to get all mushy on you. Not very manly. But, like you always said, that's us, "men!" a result of both our training? How else can you waste folks every day and sleep well at night? Emotions were always pretty far between us. All of that "suck it up" crap, "take it on the chin." Just bullshit if you ask me. Excuses to mask feelings between guys. I see it all the time here too. Nobody wants to get caught crying much less pissing their pants.

Go to the Club and suck 'em down. At these prices, who can afford not to. And free cigarettes!!! You got me covered. "Fire for effect."

But, what the hell. What can they do? Send me to Vietnam? (That's a standing joke here, Dad. I'm sure you had similar ones in the Pacific.)

Maybe we can have a beer, or better yet, a bottle of Johnny Walker Black when I get back and talk about it all.

Dad, I love you,

JR

TWELVE (LETTERS HOME)

14 October 1970

Mom, Dad,

Well, I had a suspicion that as soon as I started counting my days something would happen. Don't worry, I'm fine but I finally got my cherry REALLY popped. (Got shot down). 97 days and a wake up. But who's counting?

Hope you're sitting down for this. I had my transmission shot up the other night along Highway 13 by dinks in a sampan. Look so innocent but not! We came close for a look/see and they opened up with a .51 Cal from under some bags of rice. They call it the "Copter Killer." Fly here a while and you understand why.

It only took out my hydraulic lines and a Huey is hard to control without hydraulics. Especially trying to do evasive maneuvers, low level at night. Fortunately, the transmission or anything else didn't take any damaging rounds, just some scrapes and holes in the fuselage and we headed off up river as fast as we could. But just the shock of the Master Caution Lights flashing and the alarm sound blasting in your ears is enough to make you shit your pants. The guys in the back were freaking out to be sure.

The two gunships returned fire with pretty much everything they had. I gained some altitude and we headed to Cu Chi where we did an emergency landing. The following day, a shit-hook (Chinook) helicopter sling loaded Miss Hap back to the company area. What a cool sight, seeing her dangling there a few hundred feet below that Chinook. I got a couple of good shots of it, too. I love my Nikon and my new zoom lens. The fish-eye is next.

Next time we fly out there, I'll look to see if there is anything left there after the 105s worked the place over.

Again, don't worry I'm fine, as is my whole crew. I just wanted to be the one to tell you in case you heard about it someplace else. Always some nosy news-folks everywhere.

Not so lucky though, Lee, the kid I got assigned here with. He was shot in the leg with .51 Caliber rounds coming up through the floor on a CA north of Tay Ninh. That's where that big mountain is.

Might lose his leg. We all hope not. He's probably in Japan by now. Hope he writes. Anyway, getting shorter and shorter. You may need a magnifying glass to see me. Just don't accidentally melt me like a slug with it. Ha!

Love,

Me

PS. The gook we captured turned out to be some sort of VC Colonel or something. Also, glad to hear Jimbo's number finally came up. Joke's on him now. Wonder if he'll run.

11/14/70

Hey guys,

So far so good I guess. About 56 days and a wake up if my math is correct. But who's counting? So, I am leaving and that's that. But Lee lost the leg and may have an infection. It's almost better not knowing. I don't think I am going to write him back. Keep him guessing if he makes it. Fuck it.

Vietnamization is in full blast. In addition to VNAF copilots we have gook tower operators at many airfields. Guiding the VC in I guess. There are stories about some of the VNAF pilots flying VC and NVA around and pretending to be inserting GIs. I haven't seen it but wouldn't not believe it. Nothing can't happen here.

Gung-ho asshole lifers are now at the PX sometimes, checking combat boots for shines. We brought a few guys in from a LRRP mission for a few minutes before we had to reinsert them. They wanted to get cigarettes and some candy bars. Dickheads told them they couldn't go in. Took them around to the exit doors and the girl there let them in. Pays to have friends in high places! Trying to keep a good attitude, but it's getting harder and harder to do. All of that BS I was taught growing up. Catholic schools, Catholic upbringing. Religious rigmarole. What was that? The few guys I know that still go to Mass are full of it, too, as far as I am concerned. Go shoot a few folks one day, go to confession the next and do it all over again and again. Go to confession knowing full well you are going to go out and do it all over day after day. Can't do that. Guilt kills. Believe me. Most of the guys I know who bought it had some sort of guilt trip or superiority complex. Hard to stay "normal."

And the gooks too. They wear their Buddha charms around their necks. Put them in their mouth when they attack. Some superstition I guess, like the little white hosts. Some guys collect VC ears. Rumor is they (the gooks) believe they can't get into wherever they think they go when they die if any parts are missing or something like that. At least that's what I heard. I guess I have just plain lost faith, especially when I think of Mrs. Mrs. Laughton and Lance. What a waste.

Well, enough of this upbeat dumping all over you. Just a heads up for you in advance of my return.

Be good, love you,

JR

TWELVE (LETTERS HOME)

19 December, 1970

Hello again.

As I count down my days (too short to even mention) I took advantage of some of these down days and spent some time in Saigon visiting more than just bars and night clubs. There are some cool museums here. I had no idea. Most guys that I know just call them gooks. And they are, the ones who try to kill you that is. I mean you can't really get up the gumption to go out everyday and kill your best friends can you? So you have to sorta not really think about them as people who have lives, wives, kids, homes. But the Vietnamese, they are pretty cool. We had a couple VNAF pilots assigned to our unit and I went into Saigon with some of them a couple days ago. Everybody thought for sure that I would be secretly kidnapped and taken hostage by them. But obviously, I wasn't. That guy I mentioned before, Moon Man, he came along too. Strange guy but fun. He scored some acid and we didn't see him almost all day. We both made it back if you were wondering.

I remember in school taking an art history class and studying those Roman and Greek sculptures and buildings. But they made the same kind of stuff here too. Quite cool. I would have never guessed. All we ever see are makeshift booby traps and bamboo hootches in villages. But I am learning to see just how intricate some of the stuff they have here is. Such workmanship. Makes me really appreciate Uncle Bill's furniture. I think I might see him in a new light when I get back.

We went to lunch in the Cho Lon area of Saigon. That's where the night clubs, Saigon Tea Girls and strippers are. But we went to a traditional restaurant in an old hotel. There were a few military brass there and guys I think that were reporters with lots of cameras. Glad I had my Nikon. I fit right in.

But for the most part, Vietnamese families. It was great. Not like ordering the number 12 or number 8 in a Chinese restaurant back home. I mean it was a very nice day, hard to believe we were in a war zone. I bought you some really cool hand-carved elephants and some lacquered plates for the wall. I'll bring them home with me when I leave.

Well, today we learned we will be heading back into good ol' Cambodia. Nothing new for me! Ha! I'll still be flying nights, just further across the border. You probably heard a couple days ago… actually the day after we went to Saigon, there was a rocket attack on Bien Hoa which is literally across the street from our base. You probably hear about things like Operation Tailwind in the news there. We've been staging for something big for sure. Still hauling a lot of brass around as with my last reports. Pretty safe duty as nobody wants too many field-grade KIA in the news.

I find myself thinking, too much maybe, about home. My experiences, so different from everybody back home. Sometimes I fear I may not fit in any longer. And I surely don't fit in with the lifers in the Army. Guess I'll be a loner. My goals of flying for an airline are sorta fading too. Just sounds tedious. More uniforms and haircuts. Ready to kick back for a while. Maybe become a hippie like the rest of them. The days in Saigon have struck a chord in me. These people, living such normal-seeming lives in the middle of war. At least on the surface. How "normal" will I be sitting in a restaurant back in The World? All of the war protesters. My haircut alone will mark me as a baby-killer for sure. But I need to shut up. This melancholy bullshit is what gets guys killed. Anyway, just rambling.

So, we have this mission and then I think I will be set aside for the remaining few days. Too short to fly safely they say. Probably true. Then there was George! I hope Tailwind turns out to be just another quick in and out. Can't really belabor this point either though. Making me feel morbid. Mulling shit over too much. Anyway, we're down the totem pole a bit and only know we are going somewhere. Hope it will be fun!

More next week,

Love, Me!

TWELVE (LETTERS HOME)

Read This Last!
Don't even think about it Billy!

June 29, 2024

Jar Jar (Billy),

According to your sister, it's empowering to call you "Billy" knowing just how much you always hated being called by your actual first name. No, just "Jar Jar," that's all. You are your father's junior after all. Junior Junior… "Jr, Jr." Funny! And we always got it… just like your dad, anything but "Billy." So, today, I'm calling you Billy and you can still just call me whatever.

We came across this small pile of letters when we were cleaning out an old box of Christmas cards etc. from your grandpa's stuff that your dad still hadn't thrown out. We were kinda hoping we'd find some old money. Maybe some silver coins or, better yet, those two-dollar bills, "silver certificates," everyone used to send kids for birthdays. But no, just these letters from your dad: home from Vietnam. Brought back many memories.

With you being better known as "junior, junior," we decided you should have the duty and responsibility of being the family record holder (at least of these) until someone (or no one) else wants them. Do with them what you want. Maybe the library might want them eventually. We made photocopies and will keep them here with us. I (we) still miss your father to this day.

49

We put them in order, but there are a bunch of holes for sure and Grams always said he wrote at least twice a month. But it is what it is, and this is that. Take time to read them because they answer a lot of questions we all had over the years that none of us could ever figure out. And you might be able to use them in your next book. You know we are very proud of you, our "family author."

JR always joked about how "earning a living by getting people pissed off enough to shoot at him" was his best skill. These letters definitely opened some doors to better understanding that point of view. His eventual faith. His values, the way he would always come through for any of us right when you knew you were done for. Someday I'll tell you what he pulled off for me. I'll never forget, nor will Millie.

What a basis to operate from… the "pissing off people" thing. I always thought of it as some sort of sick humor. But these letters say something different. They really shed some light on so much "stuff" for all of us. Filled in some gaps in understanding his quick-witted, sometimes sick humor and insight. Seeing around corners as they say on detective shows. For me especially, I think the spaces between the dots have gotten smaller. I get it better now. At least I think I do.

Sorry you aren't closer to home. We would all rather be with you to share all of this in person. Funny too, reading about Jimbo. Sorta glad we never got to meet him. Everyone here in town seems to have finally come to grips that he is probably either KIA or MIA. Never to return. But the stories about his going AWOL in Nam his first month there, never to be heard from again, still abound. And I wouldn't doubt them one iota. They all still stand strong here and are almost legendary.

Your dad always said that he was such an A-hole that he would be too proud to come home after chickening out there and abandoning his guys. Flew to Thailand on a cargo plane they said and that was it. Maybe made it to Canada. Him and maybe Jenny too. What jerks. Another rumor is that she's actually that Johnson lady. Lives upstate. Your dad said he never saw her again either after coming back from Nam. Funny how people come in and out of our lives almost like cigarette smoke.

Maybe you can put some of your father's old VN photos together with some of these letters and put a bit more of that puzzle he was together for all of us. When you do, call or email us. There is always the extra room here and your old house looks almost the same. Repainted but the same.

Well, we must go for now. Gotta get the kids to those activities and, of course, church later tonight. Praying for you. We all hope you have started going again too.

Love,

Your Cousin, Frank

A Tragic Fall

by
SSgt. Jacob Parkinson

I Am the American Flag

Since the nation I represent, my Nation, has lost all sense of my idealistic protections, allow me to refresh your memory:

I am the American Flag, designed to represent a nation of freedom, hope, dreams, equality, comraderie, and brotherhood. The world's greatest warriors are bound by an oath to protect me at all costs. I love every man and woman who straps me to their uniform or salutes me as they walk by in perfect disciplined stride. I have always loved every man and woman who has defended my ideals of freedom, liberty, and democracy. People of all races and beliefs have laid down their lives in defense of my principles. I drape their coffins in my loving embrace as I say goodbye to my heroes.

The stars and stripes I proudly display are to be unleashed in battle only in the event that any nation threatens the sovereignty of the ideals or principles upheld by the citizens I am charged to protect. I am to be unfurled on those who stand on the necks of their nation's citizens and deny them the basic human rights entitled to all of mankind. That is my purpose: to ensure the pursuit of happiness, freedom, and democracy.

My standards are to be flown at half-mast for all fallen warriors. That is non-debatable. The fallen are mine, and my full solemnness and grief is theirs. They are *my* warriors to send to the afterlife, not yours. I safeguard their souls as they are laid to their peaceful rest. I am then folded and passed to the grieving loved ones, to forever comfort them through an eternity of loss.

I am to be used to blanket the weak and provide hope for those who are under the boot of tyranny. "One Nation under God, indivisible, with liberty and justice for all." Those are not mere words to me. They are sacred. I fly over every corner of this nation. I am on buildings, trucks, cars, boats, houses, clothing, and uniforms. I see a land utterly divided. I see *Liberty* stripped from my citizens like clockwork. I see no *Justice for All.*

My symbolic design is to stand against any entity, foreign or domestic, that is in direct conflict with my sovereign principles: equality, tolerance, justice, and freedom from the abuse of power for all who reside under my watchful banner. Should my vanquished enemies rise again, I shall fly proudly head first into battle to meet them.

My colors are to be flown with the noblest intentions. No exception. I do not care about politics. Do not fly me at your rallies. It is a disgrace to me and those I protect. I sit in the background of your political events, all the while listening to vapid, orange-faced politicians spew lies about what I am supposed to represent. It is appalling. I represent all who stand for democracy—true democracy.

I am not to be flown on level, and for damn sure not below any other banner, standard, or flag. That is non-negotiable. How dare you fly me on level with a banner that has some ridiculous politician's name or face emblazoned on my fabric. It is an injustice.

My colors are not to be unfurled against my own countrymen, regardless of political affiliation. I am not to be burned or trampled upon; it hurts. If you must burn me, honor me. If you must trample upon me, remember me. It is my watchful protection that puts courage in your voice to be heard. Kneel proudly, raise a fist triumphantly. I do not abandon those under my faithful banner.

Lastly, I cannot understate the importance of this next point enough: I fly proud and will not tolerate being disgraced. Do not fly me or display me if you are advancing racist ideology or the oppression of basic human rights for *all* people. If you are one of those groups who do so and display me, you are sadly mistaken as to my true purpose. I listen to your *hostile* rhetoric as I hang on your wall, fly above your house, off the back of your tailgate or your motorcycle with disgraceful exhaust burn marks and lower my head in shame. I have been draped over uniformed coffins of all races and religions, not just white coffins. Do not fly my standards if you oppose liberty and justice for all. *I am the American Flag.*

A TRAGIC FALL

'Twas the Nightmare Before Christmas 2004

'Twas the night before Christmas 2004, when all through the land

not a creature was stirring, except for the enemy coming up with a plan.

The Marines' packs hung heavily on their iron shoulders with care,

all in need of a restless sleep that seems to be rare.

The exhausted Marines were all nestled with rifles in hand,

while visions of enemy movement danced across the forsaken land.

And Culpepper with the radio attached to his strap and I, in my sweat-soaked boonie cap,

had just settled on the rooftop for a 50/50 fire watch nap.

When out from below arose such a clatter,

we sprang from our packs to see what was the matter.

Away to the edge we flew in an anger-fueled dash.

Threw on the NVGs and pointed our rifles down range in a flash.

The moon glistening off the armored vehicles all parked in a row

gave illumination to insurgents hiding down below.

When what to my tired eyes did appear

but miniature Del Vecchio and the rest of 1st squad, oh fuckin' dear.

With myself, yet lively and quick,

SSgt. JACOB PARKINSON

I knew in that moment 1st squad was the shit.
More rapid than SEALs, my squad, they came,
and I whistled and yelled and called them by name.

On *Morales* and *Thomas*, now *Del Vecchio*, on *Cooper* and
Culpepper!
Now *Delta*, on *Perry* and *Doherty*, now *Jackson* and
James!
To the side palms and atop o' the wall!
Engage them, engage them, engage them all!

As the enemy dashes, tracer rounds fly.
When adversary meets M-1 Abrams, pink mist fills the sky.
So up to other rooftops 1st squad expertly flew
with flaks full of magazines and grenades all askew.

Then a stumbling and bumbling we heard on the roof
the scurrying and running of each little insurgent's hoof.
And as I flicked my head, 1st squad was turning 'round,
down into the shit canal, I fell with a pound.
I was drenched in filth from my head to my foot,
and my cammies were all tarnished with feces and toxic
soot.

James and Culpepper would pull me out by the strap of my
pack.
I looked like a shit covered turtle, cussin' flat on my back.
My eyes, oh how they raged! My dimples, not very cherry,
my worn face buried beneath layers of shit, oh so merry.

A TRAGIC FALL

1st squad moved on clearing buildings, quick as an arrow
loosed from a bow.
We, tired Grunts, moved with heroic purpose up IED row.
The windswept sand held tight in the grit of their teeth,
the smoke from the M-1 Abrams encircled their heads like
a Christmas wreath.

Their platoon commander had a broad face and a little
round belly
that shook when he laughed, like a bowl full of gutless
jelly.
He was chubby and plump, less a Marine, more like an elf.
I laughed when I saw him, in spite of myself.

After an explosion, the platoon commander went right to
his cowardly work,
filling the airwaves with a suicidal command; man, what a
fuckin' jerk.
With a crazy wink of his eye, an evil order flew from his
head
that soon made me realize 1st squad had everything to
dread.

I tried to keep my steely-eyed pose,
And with a slight nod, Delta arose.
I relayed the terrible commotion as my men began to bristle
And away the squad flew, following their leader like a
heat-seeking missile.
1st squad had had enough, and proclaimed as they
disappeared from sight:
"Fuck no, not this goddamn night!"

SSgt. JACOB PARKINSON

58

The Unsung

It's brutal. It's exhausting. The hours are long and there is no pay.

It's the one job no one wants, but those who have it are so very proud.

You are on call 24/7. You must be therapist and best friend.

You are thrown into the role of an emotional dumping ground.

You weather storm after storm until the calm and then the warmth of a breakthrough.

You see us off with a smile and a tear and welcome us home with the same. It is these fleeting moments of warm smiles and loving tears we share that belong only to you.

You offer the solace of unwavering support that is unfairly placed upon the strength of your unyielding shoulders.

The outside world applauds us, but you, the inside world, can see beneath the armor. There is weakness in us, and from that daunting weakness springs your compassion.

There are no parades for you. No medals or ribbons adorn your chest. No headlines of your bravery, which you display every desperate day.

There is no "Thank you for your service" when out in public. We, the Veterans, know that *thanks* belongs to you.

You have the most daunting MOS in the military: *the loved one.*

You are *The Unsung…* that needs to change.

~SSgt. Jacob Parkinson

Saga of the Walking Wounded

To whom it may concern,

We can be numb, emotionless, distant, and angry at times. The human brain is not designed to handle the sensory overload that each one of us has endured during our combat tours. The actions experienced in true combat dramatically rewire and reprogram our brains. This leads Combat Veterans to experience a variety of emotions and symptoms not relatable to the civilian world. It is not an excuse or a free pass, it is our own personal Hell.

Somewhere in the blackness we still have true emotions, but they are hidden from your view in a dark, bottomless abyss. We are still human, dealing with inhuman actions and experiences. The loss of our *purpose* in this ever-changing and growing world has left each one of us dangling and exposed. Nothing in life can give us the pride we felt fighting alongside our brothers in the most hellish of situations.

We do not share our stories except with fellow combatants and even then, it's just a flash of what each of us has experienced. Each warrior's story has the same daunting similarity, regardless of the theater of combat: action, chaos, anger, sadness, and most importantly, brotherhood. To look at the man at your three, six, nine, and twelve o'clock positions and know he will not fail.

We haunted few withdraw into ourselves not to push you away, but to process that permanent loss of overwhelming pride and purpose. We withdraw to remember those brothers we have lost and those that fought alongside us, who chewed that same hellish dirt. When we succumb to our memories, it is nothing against your love for us. It is our way to process and remember. These moments of honor and remorse are not meant to hurt or ignore your gentle, loving touch.

As much as each one of these men are heroes and honorable warriors, they are nothing without your strength, love, understanding and support. You, *the loved ones,* are the true and unheralded heroes of our wars that have been lost in society's misunderstanding of combat fatigue. Your mental strength, day in and day out, is a mental strength that we, war-fighters, will never fathom or achieve. We, Walking Wounded, would be lost to our despair and unrelenting anguish without your support and ironclad determination to see us through.

Our combat experiences are ours and ours alone. It is a burden that will haunt us for an eternity. It is something we feel will crush your beautiful spirit and we so desperately want to protect you from that terrible burden. You, *the loved ones,* are the lighthouse in the fog that will guide us back to safety. Do not panic during our fogs; we always find our way back to the embracing light you radiate, and for that we are so very grateful. We can never repay you for your devotion and compassion; we can only offer a humbled, *Thank you for your service.*

Ode to the Listeners

They listen without judgment or reprisal from their bland, government-issued desk.

These unnoticed listeners provide support, encouragement, solace, escape, and protection.

We, the Veterans, complain, decompress, vent, rant, cry, isolate, and deflate all before them, yet there is no disgust or fear from the *listeners*.

The *listeners* are steadfast and unwavering in their care for us, the walking wounded. The *listeners* absorb all of our troubles, trauma, crises, and the most detrimental of all: our hopelessness and our despair.

We leave their presence after dumping our fears, regrets, shame, experiences, and guilt onto those shoulders of iron.

What becomes of these stoic *listeners* at the end of the trying day?

Who is there to listen to them at day's end, for they are bound by confidentiality?

Who consoles those compassionate *listeners* when the day's absorption of trauma overwhelms their brave levees?

No allowance for relief or decompression.

The *listeners* must do what they plead for us Veterans never to do: *compartmentalize*.

And when the dreaded happens and that somber call comes forth to the *listener*:

One of their warriors has fallen, succumbing to their battle against that ever present hopelessness, the *listeners'* sacred desire to save… shattered.

That is the *listeners'* biggest fear: that lonely, dreaded call. The *listeners* fight day and night, never wavering in this battle to save us wounded, from the unrelenting darkness and our self-defeating manifestations.

Who puts a comforting hand on the *listener* and compassionately begs *move forward, remember the past, but move forward. Do not despair, there is still hope, please believe me.*

Who sits with the *listeners* in an office and comforts them as the ghost of another fallen warrior drifts to the surface and eases through the cracks in their gallant, brave armor?

The *listener*, unable to use their formidable skills to keep the loss at bay, succumbs to that tidal wave of grief quietly, privately.

No, the *listener* must do this *alone*. Without a comforting hand.

They will never quit, even against the most dreaded of odds, those stoic *listeners*.

Round after round, round after round, round after round. Until the day is finally over. Only to repeat the next.

Who are these people, these selfless, brave *listeners?* We Veterans call them docs, clinicians, therapists, nurses, social workers. But most of all we call them *Angels*.

We, troubled Veterans, leave and walk away with a rushed and haggard "Thanks, Doc." Our heads down walking away, back turned, we know you wonder in the dark recesses, *will you see us again?* I give this promise to you, our *listener*, you will.

Flip the Switch

The grass is bright green, the open West Texas sky a brilliant, cloudless blue. The weather is perfect. I stare up at the beauty through my facemask, laying sprawled on the soft earth. I feel the vibrations of concussive footsteps thundering towards me. "Shit," I grumble under my gasping breath. He arrives. I rise before him, humbled, and then it begins.

"Goddamnit Parks, you need to put that runnin' back on his ass! What's wrong with you?!"

The needed oxygen fills my lungs once more and I think to myself, *what* is *wrong with me?* but say nothing and await more of the verbal onslaught.

"Goddamnit, you have all the talent and speed in the world but can't put it together, son. You need to learn to flip the switch and become an animal out there, a fuckin' monster!" My helmet sinks further into my chest. He's right. I can only offer a subdued, "Yes, sir."

***

Night is stifling in the southern California summer heat; the planes from the San Diego International Airport make their familiar whining deceleration and acceleration onto and off of the unforgiving tarmac. It is a sound that stokes longing in every Marine recruit in that hot, suffocating squad bay: the longing for the day each can board one of those escaping planes to anywhere but here. A tall, granite Marine drill instructor glides across the gleaming, mirror-like floor so painstakingly polished by the recruits. The drill instructor walks with steely purpose amongst the recruits as they freeze with fear in their racks. The older Marine smiles wickedly. It is finally his time alone with the petrified recruits.

"Ears!" he commands deeply.

"Open, sir!" the young recruits bellow in unison.

"This is for all you shit-stains that are goin' infantry, the rest of you are worthless fucks, got that?!" The old, tired Marine growls, his deep voice betraying twenty-six long years of hardened service to the nation.

Another round of an obedient, "Yes, sir!" echoes forth from the dark squad bay.

The old war horse continues, "You don't know what it's like to have the enemy sneak up on your foxhole and put a knife to your throat. You don't know what it's like to have an enemy put a rifle in your face, do you?!"

The infantry recruits respond, petrified, "No, sir!"

The drill instructor continues his effortless glide around the squad bay, like the *boogeyman* looking for a trembling child to scare into never-ending nightmares. "What do you do?"

It is rhetorical. Not a quivering soul answers; the barracks are deathly silent, as if the whole base of infantry recruits awaits the horrific answer to their perilous future.

"You infantry Marines, you grunts, better learn to flip the switch and become nothing but a goddamn killin' machine! If not, you are dead. Got that?"

This is not rhetorical. We, destined infantry Marines, sound off as loud as our immature lungs allow: "Yes sir!"

***

Flames soar to dramatic heights in the starry night sky, casting their orange glow upon the cluster of ground pounders below. They are shocked and bewildered, each soldier trying and failing to find the words to describe what they're witnessing. The screams of the dying echo across the unforgiving desert landscape, yet the witnessing Marines are helpless to intervene, to save lives. They are designed only to take life. The ball of fire laughs cruelly at the young grunts, mocking their shock and trauma as its flames mercilessly consume their men, friends, and brothers in arms.

The agony of the dying slowly fades away as the fire continues to rage over the smoldering wreckage. Faced with their own mortality, the surviving Marines slowly congregate to support one another in isolated silence. Command has arrived on the desolate scene. The weary infantry Marines receive their orders, and it is a terrifying demand for the young survivors.

"Get on a helicopter again."

The survivors' eyes go wide with terror and look to me to intervene. *I* have nothing for them. Command senses the fear and hesitation.

"Sgt. Parks, a word," the first sergeant bellows for all to hear. "Is this horrific? It sure the fuck is. Does this stop you from being a Marine? No it does fucking not. Get these men on the bird and let's go home. You need to flip the switch and move forward, Sgt. Parks. You all do."

I reply emotionlessly, a trained machine: "Yes sir."

***

"Men, this will be the single largest urban battle since the Vietnam War. It's time to do what we were made to do.

Let's go get some!" Our battalion commander's booming war cry echoes throughout our staging area.

It's time. *Operation Phantom Fury*. The mission is simple: eliminate all enemy personnel in and around the war-torn city of Fallujah. This is what Marine infantry is designed for: *any clime, any place*. After the war speech, I walk amongst my young warriors as they fill magazines with lethal ammunition, adjust their gear so it feels just right on the move, and write their last letters home: final goodbyes to loved ones should Death come calling. It is time for my speech, a speech that will be given by many a grizzled squad leader to his men on the eve of a knowing battle. My young Marines look up from their intense preparation, wide-eyed and full of adrenaline.

"Men, I'm not going to give you some rah-rah bullshit speech. Tomorrow, we have a job to do and a responsibility to every man in this squad: bring each other home. What I need from you men is simple: flip the switch and become emotionless fuckin' door-kickin' machines. We stop for nothing until the job is done. Let's go to work."

Not caring what was in store for us all, my men blindly, faithfully respond "Yes sir!"

***

Flashing red and blue lights descend upon me like a wave of dispensing justice. I fall down drunk with the unforgiving handcuffs reflecting the shine of the overhead street lamp, clamping around my wrists in deserved pain. The cold, heavy steel cage door slides into its locked position with a loud, jarring *clunk*. Sinking against the frozen concrete wall, the thought comes barreling towards my drunken consciousness. *How did you let things come to this, you piece of shit?* The hangover begins to set in, along with the despair and uncontrollable rage.

The old, graying, tired guard stops and looks in with soulful pity. "You shouldn't be in here, Marine. It's time to flip the switch and come on home, son."

I keep my head low in grueling shame. "Yes sir."

***

The darkness creeps in slowly from the sides, like the fading of an old black and white movie scene. It is this darkness that is most welcome for the old, tired, broken Marine. The Darkness does not judge or console. It gives no encouragement or promise of a better future. No, the Darkness is there for remembrance, guilt, remorse, pain, grief, failure, and the all-consuming regret. The infantry Marine is tired of fighting off the Dark, with its ability to isolate and drown, bombarding him with constant images of an unforgiving past. The bottle sits next to his trigger finger. He pulls another solemn drink. The pills sit next to his magazine quick pull hand. The calloused palmful of white tablets fly smoothly down with the clear, piss-warm vodka.

The Darkness takes a seat at the empty dining room table with the combat infantry Marine. It smiles confidently and asks, "What's next, SSgt. Parks?"

I answer the dark curse nonchalantly. "What the fuck do you think, Devil?"

Darkness smiles. It knows it has won. "Please enlighten."

I look the menacing specter in its wicked, cold eyes. "Time to flip the switch and go dark."

Darkness leans back in the chair with a gloating, cruel smile. "Yes sir."

That Sparkle

"I remember when you were just a little thing, running buck naked in the backyard, not a care in the world. Even when you ran head first into the cactus, with all that crying and caterwauling, you had this sparkle in your eye, son. I don't know what it was, but as I said my *oh poor baby*, and tried to console you in your pain, that sparkle made me realize, my son, that you were destined for great, beautiful things." The loving mother looks upon her grown Marine.

He does not answer. Her Marine remains stoic and reserved.

"Do you remember the time you hit an in-the-park home run in little league?"

There is no reply for the frail, loving mother.

"No? Well, I do. You were so fast, turning those little bases. The other parents all looked to me with astonishment as you ran like a West Texas Jackrabbit, only to be called out at home plate. I was so upset, as any proud mother would be, but I didn't have to get up and argue. Before I knew, the other parents had stormed the field with the coach, surrounding that poor umpire with a bunch of expletives." The loving mother emits a tiny, tired chuckle into the gray, quiet, troublesome day. "You came storming over to the dugout with the maddest little face. All you said to me through the chain-link fence was, 'I was safe, Mama.' And there it was, that wonderful *sparkle*—flashing with an intense little anger, but it persisted. I was so proud of you in that moment, son. I just knew you were destined for great, beautiful things."

He does not answer. Her Marine remains stoic and reserved, staring into a dark void that only he can see. The fall nip in the air bites into the frail woman's old bones as she wraps her coat tighter around her small torso.

"Do you remember your last track meet? Regionals?"

Her Marine still offers no response.

"I do. It was one of the few I could get to. You ran the fastest split on the team. I loved watching you run, son. You were so graceful with your speed but ran with an unbridled intensity. It was you against everyone who said you couldn't keep up. You loved proving people wrong with your unexpected speed. As your number one supporter, I enjoyed seeing their shocked expressions. You made me so proud. You always made me proud, son. You came off the track beaming, your coach and teammates all patting you on the shoulders. It was then I saw that sparkle in your eyes from across the football field. I can never miss my boy's sparkle. 'My son is destined for great, beautiful things'… my only prideful thought."

He does not answer. Her Marine remains stoic and reserved, the only way he knows. His bearing never wavers.

"I remember the night you came and told me you were leaving for the Marine Corps. Do you?" The older woman looks about, hoping for an answer that does not arrive. "No? I was working the night shift at the postal center, and the security guard had to come grab me to tell me I had a visitor. It was almost midnight, son. Remember?" She pauses for a second, trying to garner the strength to continue the memory.

"I was so scared as I walked out the front door into the pitch-black night, and you were smiling from ear to ear. You felt as if you were answering some deep instinctual calling— a calling no mother can stop, no matter how hard we try. 'I'm leavin' for the Marines. I'm goin' to make you so proud,

Mama.' And there it was, that magnificent sparkle in your eyes, on fire with intense pride. I watched you disappear into the night to become an infantry Marine. A mother's tears fell in that lonely, dark parking lot, son. I knew you were destined for great, beautiful, and horrible things."

He does not answer. Her Marine remains stoic and reserved, the only way he knows. His emotions vacated long ago; he feels nothing, not even the bitter cold.

"The day you left the Marines, I thought *finally my boy is coming home.* You were leaving just in time; the War on Terror was beginning for our country. That night you came to visit all those years ago, I knew something was amiss, my son. A mother always knows. You told me the Marines called you back and you were going to war, every mother's worst fear. My world stopped then, son. I truly didn't know if I would be able to speak, and then I saw that sparkle in your eyes filled with calling, duty, bravery, and rage. A mother stood no chance against that passion and longing for honor and service. You tried to reassure me that you were too good a squad leader to die, and you would be home soon. That sparkle in your eye was a raging forest fire and it scared me, my son. My only thought was, *my son is destined for horrible, brutal things.*

He does not answer. Her Marine remains stoic and reserved, letting his broken mother's words fill the surrounding air with heavy, solemn confession.

"You kept your word, my boy, you came home. And yet, what came home was not the boy I pulled from the cactus, not my little leaguer, or my track star, and not even the boot camp honor man who never stopped smiling on graduation day. No, what came home was a tired, worn, reluctant, displaced young man who didn't know if he belonged here in the land of the living or with the fallen warriors left behind on the battlefield. My beautiful boy, aged well beyond his years. Do you remember when your sister and I came to visit when you arrived back at base?"

There remains nothing but silence from the steadfast Marine.

"No? We surely do. It was instantaneous. When your sister and I laid our tearful, joyous eyes on you, we froze. Your petrified sister whispered to me, 'That's not Jake anymore, Mama.' I looked upon you, my son, with all the motherly intuition and love humanly possible, and I saw that sparkle—that glimmer of hope, promise, humor, understanding, and compassion—was gone. Your eyes were vacant, cold, and dark. Your sparkle was extinguished by hate, anger, grief, sorrow, and the most damaging, regret. I almost died that day, my beautiful boy. My only horrible thought, *I have lost my son forever* as I latched onto you for a hug that seemed so forced from you. My son, you wanted no part of being home and I should have realized then that you will never truly be home. I never saw that bright, gorgeous sparkle in your eyes again. Oh, my baby boy, you did such great and beautiful things. Your men still send me stories of your time together over there. It makes me wonder, did your men ever get to see that joyous sparkle in your eyes, to know under your guidance and watch they would be okay? Did your sparkle give them solace and courage for what must come next? I hope it did, my son."

He does not answer. Her Marine remains stoic and reserved, waiting for his visitor to finish her sentiments, like all the others who come to see him.

The small, frail, older woman then slowly stands, pushing herself up with the assistance of the cold, smooth, granite tombstone. She wraps the scarf around her neck tighter to fight off the bitter cold of the day. The doting mother looks down lovingly at the military grave marker, then she rests her fragile, bony hand gently atop the chiseled memorial; her tears fall upon the cold, hardy stone and shimmer in the pale light. "I hope you found your sparkle again, and are seeing such great, beautiful things. Rest easy, my son."

The Accident

by
Benjamin Fortier

September, 2005

Jerri's cell phone buzzed. She stopped pushing her grocery cart to fish it from her pocket.

LIVVY, her phone alerted her.

"Hey hun, what's up?" Jerri continued past an aromatic display of herbs.

"Mom!"

Jerri stopped in her tracks. There was fear in her daughter's voice.

"What's going on, Liv?"

"It's Dad. He was in a crash."

Jerri's stomach lurched. "What?"

"Cameron just called. He said you didn't pick up. He saw it all happen in the car behind Dad." Olivia sobbed.

Jerri checked her phone and confirmed there were multiple missed calls from Cameron.

"Do you know where he is?" Jerri deserted her cart and headed toward the exit of the market.

"The Veterans Hospital."

"Okay, I'm going there now."

"Please call me."

"I will, honey. We will get through this, okay?"

"Yeah."

Jerri fumbled with her keys. Her hands felt hot against the steering wheel. A thin bead of sweat began running down the side of her head. She imagined Arthur on a gurney, wheeled through the hospital corridors, a nurse performing chest compressions hard enough to break his ribs.

Start the car.

She focused on her breath. It was shaky. Her inhales and exhales jittered. Still, she remained intent on grounding herself.

We need to get out of here. Start the car and go.

In defiance, she kept her eyes shut, focusing on her breathing exercise. After a few cycles, the shaking dissipated. She felt grounded and more in control of her body. She slowly opened her eyes, staring out at the rows of cars through the windshield of her SUV. For a moment, it felt quiet. There was no humming of the engine or music on the radio. Even the noise in her mind seemed to be temporarily muted.

"Fuck." She sighed, starting the vehicle.

***

Jerri scurried through the hospital entrance and followed the signs to the Emergency Department's waiting room. As soon as she made eye contact with Cam, he stood and they embraced.

"How are you doing?" She stepped back and examined his face.

"I'm fine. Nothing happened to me."

"What *did* happen, Cam?"

He sat back down heavily as if the weight of the memory sank him. He sighed, combing his hands through his wavy chestnut hair. She sat next to him and listened.

"I was following Arthur to the driving range. We'd just gotten lunch. I was in the lane next to Art's, but behind him by a few car lengths. I noticed something in the road ahead of us, and it was getting closer and closer really fast. I realized it was someone going the wrong way on the highway, so I swerved into the breakdown lane. Arthur…"

Cameron shook his head, tears building up in the corner of his eyes. She grasped his hand and squeezed in reassurance. He looked to the floor.

"There was this massive explosion. Like someone flying overhead dropped a bomb in the middle of the highway. I just remember seeing the guy who hit Art running across the highway. I couldn't even see Art through all the smoke. I thought nobody could survive that, that I was looking at his deathbed, but they cut him out while I was giving the police a statement. I couldn't believe it."

"God, Cam. I'm so sorry you had to see that," she said. "Did they catch the guy who hit him?"

"I don't know. As soon as I could, I followed the ambulance here. The police were still looking for him when we left. He abandoned his car in the middle of the highway. I mean, I don't know if he was drunk or what."

"They'll find him, Cam. When they catch that son-of-a-bitch, we will nail him to the wall. Okay? Did you meet with anyone when you got here?"

"The doctor, yeah. He said he would take good care of Uncle Art," Cameron said. He wiped the tears that remained and steadied himself.

"Did they say when we can see him?" Jerri asked.

"They'll come and get us when they're ready. They said it'll be a few hours."

"Come with me to pick up Livvy," she said, rising out of her seat. "It won't do us any good sitting here ruminating. We can ruminate in my car."

As they exited the hospital, Jerri hoped that she was projecting an aura of confidence. Together, they headed back to Chepachet to meet with Olivia.

***

Arthur and Jerri had purchased their home in 1989—a year before Olivia entered their lives. It was on the first floor of a three-story corner lot apartment building in the historic downtown district. At the time, Arthur worked odd jobs and Jerri was senior waitstaff at a family-owned restaurant. Olivia turned their lives upside down, and the home became part office, part nursery, and a kitchen that never seemed clean. Most nights, Jerri was passed out on the couch while Arthur came in at unusual hours. His diligence in taking care of their daughter was never questioned, but when Jerri would rise the next morning, he was already gone. As she pushed open the door, Olivia looked up from her phone and rushed to hug her mother.

Jerri sighed deeply and nurtured the moment with her precious daughter.

"Cam, if you'd be a gentleman, put on the coffee." Jerri said. She needed a moment alone with Olivia.

"Sure thing." He walked into the kitchen.

"It'll be okay, honey," Jerri breathed.

Before long, the coffee machine alerted them with a high-pitched chirping followed by the clanking of ceramic mugs.

80

"Cam, let's use the travel mugs," Jerri called. "We should get back to the hospital."

As he shifted his task, his eyes glanced at a hanging picture of himself, Arthur, Jerri, and a young Olivia at the local ice skating rink. Cameron had just played his first high school game as the goalie, and Arthur was the assistant coach. The pride on his face reminded him that they had won with a shutout.

Jerri and Olivia broke their embrace when Cameron returned. "Cam, you were there? What happened?" Olivia asked, her voice thick with tears.

Cam's eyes widened. "Um," he said. He made eye contact with Jerri, and after she nodded, Cameron repeated the story about the accident on the way to the hospital.

"So there's still some hope. He can get through this," Livvy said when he was finished.

"Of course, honey. Once we get there, we will meet with the doctor right away. He'll tell us everything they've done to help Dad. He's been here tons of times, you know? It's like a new appointment every week it seems."

Livvy nodded and looked out the passenger window. Reality blurred as they sped toward fate.

***

The family didn't have to wait long to see the doctor at the hospital.

"Hi folks, I'm Dr. Crane. I'm really sorry you're going through this right now. Arthur is currently in a stable condition, but there are some things we need to talk about. If you wouldn't mind, just follow me." He escorted them through the labyrinth of the hospital, where they finally ended up in a room that seemed to be designed for conferences, outfitted with two large tables, chairs, and a presentation area with a screen for displaying media.

"This is weird," Livvy whispered to Cam.

"As I said, Mr. Bailey is currently in critical condition."

"Wait, you said he was in stable condition?" Jerri interrupted.

"Yes, I'm sorry for the confusion. We decided to stabilize him. Unfortunately, he is in critical condition after the accident."

Jerri raised her hand to her face.

"Did you say, 'We decided to stabilize him'? What other options are there when you intake a patient here?"

"Dr. Crane, you don't have to answer that."

Jerri turned to see a red-haired woman in a maroon blazer enter the room.

"Hello, everyone," the newcomer said. "My name is Carol Taylor. I am the Director of Ethical Oversight for Valor Health Administration." She tapped a laminated badge clipped to her blazer. It was embossed with a golden silhouette of an eagle and the initials VHA. "It is with our utmost, sincere apologies that we must burden you further with difficult decisions regarding your husband."

Jerri was stunned. "We don't even have a plan for my husband, who is dying right now. Maybe we should start there?"

"That's exactly where I would like to start, too, Mrs. Bailey," Carol said. "Your husband is not a registered patient at our facility. We noticed that he had a veteran's identification card. When we scanned it, it came up as a forgery. What is interesting is that we found this."

Carol pulled out a small electronic tablet. She pressed a button on the device, and an image appeared on the screen at the head of the room.

"What is this?" Jerri asked.

"It's a discharge document," Cameron said as he approached it.

"That's correct. This is your husband's discharge document, Mrs. Bailey," Carol said.

Cameron seemed drawn to the screen, like a moth to a flame.

"What does it say, Cam?" Jerri asked.

"Discharge type: Bad Conduct. Date: 11 November 1974," he said. "Veteran's Day. He got drafted—we knew that—but this says he only did two years in the Army. 1972, basic training in Georgia. That makes sense. His initial job was radio operator, then he… Oh, this is weird. He reported for special forces evaluation in the winter of '73, then returned to his home unit after a few weeks. Come the spring of '74, he got kicked out on a bad conduct." Cameron studied the document and shook his head.

"Mom?" Livvy asked with concern.

Jerri was confused. "What does any of this even mean? He told us that he had been in for much longer than that. There's got to be some kind of mistake."

"I'm afraid there is no mistake," Carol said. She switched the tablet off and pulled the device in front of her chest as if to shield herself from the hate that smoldered from Jerri. "And I'm afraid that we do not treat patients who are not in the VHA system. So we have to determine a course of action here."

Dr. Crane awkwardly stepped into the conversation.

"Please rest assured that we have done all we can to ensure your husband's safety and comfort," he added.

Carol remained detached and robotic. "We noticed that your husband has no final will or testament, further complicating things."

"Fuck," Jerri whispered to her daughter. "I told him to take care of that."

"Dr. Crane has drawn up some recommendations for Mr. Bailey. What we can promise is that once this has been sorted out, we will move forward with care and determine how it will be paid for since your husband is not an eligible VHA patient."

Carol's watch buzzed and she looked down at her wrist. "Is there anything else I can do for you?"

"Yeah, this has been super helpful." Olivia hissed.

Carol ignored her. "I'll let you and the care team work out these initial steps. We have your contact information and will be in touch."

Her heels clicked on the linoleum floor as she exited. Cameron remained in a trance, gazing at where the document had been projected.

"Can I get a minute with my family, please?" Jerri asked the doctor, who was nervously shifting in place.

He nodded, and she led Cameron and Olivia into the hallway.

"Cam, was all of that true?" Jerri hushed.

"We saw it right from the source. It doesn't make any sense that they would show us fake documents. They have to be real."

Cameron paced in a small area of the hallway. "Arthur washed out of the special forces tryouts. And he joined in 1972?"

"It feels like my head is getting pulled apart." Olivia groaned and slid down the hospital wall.

"There has to be some kind of explanation for this. Maybe there's something at home we can find. Some records. Just to have something to compare to," Jerri said.

"What about the filing cabinet? And that shoe box," Olivia added.

"Exactly what I was thinking," Jerri said.

They returned to the room where Dr. Crane waited for them with a binder filled with paperwork and forms.

"These need to be filled out and returned by this evening. If you want to go home and refresh, we will have Arthur in his room by the time you get back. Visiting hours are until ten."

Jerri took the paperwork and agreed. They followed the doctor back through the maze of corridors, where nurses and patients bustled about. As they navigated the parking lot, Cameron's vehicle chirped as it disarmed.

"Well, I'm going to head home. It'll be good to shower and clear my mind after all this."

"Cam," Jerri sighed and hugged him tightly. "This will be tough, but we'll get through it. Together."

His lips trembled as she spoke. Olivia looked at him and saw the tears build in his eyes. She turned away, and he wept into Jerri's shoulder for a moment. Jerri rubbed his back to soothe him. Cameron regained his composure and pulled away from his dear friend.

"I'll be OK. Thank you both."

"Give us a call tonight, Cam," Olivia said as they watched him open his car door.

"Of course." He smiled.

As Cameron entered the vehicle, he was hit by a waft of a unique aroma from a tree-shaped deodorizer. As he settled into the seat, his mind was transported to a time when he would overfill the interior of his car with these air fresheners to hide the smell of burnt tobacco and cannabis. He was a senior at Ponaganset High School. Arthur showed up at the diner where he worked and recalled stories about his days in the service.

***

Arthur casually leaned back in his chair. It creaked under his weight. He had just explained to Cameron how brave his father was in combat. He had seen it firsthand when they were dropped into the jungles of Cambodia on a black op—an even more secretive and deadly level of irregular warfare.

"When we pushed out of the camp, there were fourteen prisoners altogether. That was a lot more than the briefing had anticipated, but we couldn't leave them behind, Cam. Your father, he looked at me and said, 'We've got to get these Americans home.' So, that's what we did. It took nearly half the day to get 'em all out. Each time the chopper landed, we got swarmed and had to fight our way out. Your father and I both were shot up good, but we kept fighting. And they just kept coming," Arthur said.

Cameron's mouth hung agape as he heard the story. He hadn't known his dad, Maxwell Gibbons. He died soon after Cam was born. When he was fourteen, he met Arthur and finally felt like he had a father figure in his life. He was stunned to discover that Arthur had known and served with his dad.

His head rushed, excited to get to know his father outside of pictures or letters. "What was he like after the battle?"

"Drugged up from the morphine." Arthur laughed and signaled the closest server for a refill. "But proud. Real proud. He was a man who didn't think about himself. Only others. I remember our last mission together."

"You were there when he died?" Cameron asked.

"I was among the last people to see him alive, Cam. It's horrible, what happened that day. God rest his soul. He went down swingin' though, son. I tell you, he must have dropped about twenty-nine of those bastards before they got him."

Cameron became overwhelmed with a connection to Arthur that he never imagined. It was as if this stranger had entered his life to become a conduit to his father's lost mythos. These stories poured out of Arthur as Cam pried. Photos emerged. Arthur and Max on a helicopter together. Out on patrols with rifles and tactical gear. Arthur was particularly proud of his photo with the Secretary of Defense in 1980.

"That man was a hard charger, I tell you. He did us right each and every time we asked. He gave your father that Silver Star."

Long before they had met, Cameron had scoured his father's pictures, envisioning himself in tiger-striped camouflage carrying a fully automatic carbine through the jungles of Southeast Asia. His inspiration to follow in his father's footsteps intensified as he poured over the new pictures.

Cameron felt emboldened one afternoon as the pair lazily finished lunch at a restaurant.

"I've been thinking about it and want to be like you. And my dad. I talked to the Ranger recruiter last week. He told me I could sign up on a special contract."

"The Rangers? Maybe you should tone it down a bit."

"W—what do you mean?"

"They're an elite-level unit. You are… you." Arthur wiped gravy from his face. "When was the last time you did anything elite, Cam?"

Cameron shifted. "The recruiter said I could train. I'm still young. I can get strong."

Arthur sighed and looked down at the floor. "You gave up on getting strong. All this time, you should have been making something of yourself, but nah."

Cameron searched the room as if answers would appear in the wood paneling and yellowed menus. Arthur had always been his champion, except when the military came up. As soon as Cam showed interest in volunteering, Arthur had to chop it down and degrade his dreams.

"The outfit we were in was hand-picked. Selected from the top infantry units. If you aren't going to be a grunt, you might as well just go to college. Learn a trade," Arthur said.

"I have what it takes," Cameron said.

"Cam, you don't have a violent bone in your body. You're better off just staring at computer screens all day. That's what you're good at, anyway. Don't try and get into a man's world. You just won't fit in." Arthur pushed his plate aside and fished money out of his pocket. He tossed a couple of dollars down and stood.

"I'm going home. I'll see you around."

Just like that, Arthur was a stranger.

"Yeah. See you," Cam said.

***

Jerri pulled a shoe box out from under the bed. It contained pictures and memorabilia Arthur claimed were from his past life. They seemed to be the only connection to his days in Georgia and the military. Jerri believed him when he told her he was born and raised there and moved to Rhode Island in 1980. Until the day of the accident, she never questioned his motivation to escape from that part of the country. She suspected it was to run away from a life that no longer suited him. She related because she had been in that situation once before.

Guilt weighed down on her. She was ashamed she gave her heart away to a callous narcissist. When they purchased their home in Chepachet, she was elated to escape her family problems. A family with their own gauntlets of alcoholism, abuse, and perversion. It took sixteen years to realize she had only transferred her trauma somewhere else, packed up alongside the priceless, sentimental material goods.

"Find anything?" Olivia leaned against the doorway of Jerri's bedroom.

She looked at her beautiful girl. They had similar hair that grew as bouncy curls. The web of Olivia's long curls engulfed her head like a crown. Their hazel eyes locked.

"What?" Olivia asked.

"Just admiring how pretty you are," Jerri replied.

Olivia looked away, embarrassed. "Gross, Mom."

"I found Dad's box of stuff. Want to take a peek with me?"

"Sure." Livvy sat on the bed.

Jerri joined her and opened the shoe box. On the very top of the pile of trinkets was a picture of Jerri and Arthur dressed to the nines, with Arthur in a military dress uniform. An assortment of multicolored ribbons adorned his chest. Silver badges in the shapes of rifles, parachutes, torches, and shields decorated his green uniform. They stood in front of the American flag and a lit backdrop. Jerri smirked and held it up for them both to see.

"Oh my," she said.

"Whoa, Mom. Look at you guys," Olivia gushed. "Where was that?"

"That was at a country club a few years before you were born. It was a local Veteran's Day event. Military people from all over the state were there. It was the first time I saw your Dad in uniform. I was smitten, to say the least."

"That mustache…"

"I know. It was a thing back then."

***

The autumn of 1987. Rhode Island's leaves developed into shades of auburn, yellow, and orange. Jerri and Arthur had been dating for a few months. She was intrigued when he asked her to attend the Veteran's Day ball.

"A ball?" she laughed as they spoke on the phone. Images of a Cinderella-esque scene with beautiful women and men floating around a dance floor flitted through her mind.

"Yeah, everyone gets dressed up, and we shoot the shit and have dinner," Arthur said. "It's at the Shimmering Lake

90

Golf Course in Glendale. I'd love to have you as my partner for it."

Her cheeks flushed. It had been years since someone swooned over her. She wrapped the phone cord around her index finger.

"Alright," she said softly. "Let's do it. I'll get a dress."

"Great! You're going to look marvelous."

That weekend, Jerri teamed up with her college friend Deirdre to shop at a clothing store in Providence. The boutique was a small shop flanked by massive department stores.

"So tell me about this guy," Deirdre said around her gum as they lazily browsed the purses. "He must really like you to be taking you to this fancy event."

"He does! And he's great," Jerri replied. "He's a bit older, but I don't mind."

"How old?" Deirdre stopped chewing.

"Mid-thirties?"

"I've done it." Deirdre continued browsing.

"We met around here, actually. I was grabbing coffee at Roast Island before work."

"Horrible name."

"I know. Their pastries are amazing, though. So we full-on bump into each other. I knocked his frickin' drink right out of his hand. And he was just super endearing about it. Wicked apologetic. He seemed to know the entire staff there. They just gave him another coffee without any questions. I saw him there a few more times, and we just got to catching up."

"Hot?"

Jerri gave her a side-eye and coy smile. "You'll have to meet him in person and find out."

"Oh, come on. You don't have a picture of him?"

"I don't carry around pictures of guys I just met. You have to be a boyfriend for two, maybe three years, minimum."

"Yikes. That's basically a marriage time frame for me."

"Looking for something?" an elderly employee asked them politely.

"Oh," Jerri was a bit startled. "Yeah, I'm going to an event. A ball. I'm looking for something that would match a military uniform."

"A military uniform." The woman tapped her chin. "Army? Navy?"

"Army."

"Of course. I'm sure we have something for you."

Jerri's fingers trailed along the row of dresses as the helpful lady scampered off. She stopped at a deep blue gown with sequins along the halter strap. She pulled it off the rack and sized herself up.

"Hey, Dee! Take a look at this one." Jerri called out across the store.

Deirdre's head popped up from behind a stack of clutches.

She hurried over. "What'd you find?"

Jerri proudly pressed the dress against her body, and her friend stared.

"How do you do it?" Deirdre asked.

"Do what?"

"You just find the perfect thing the first time. Every time."

Jerri beamed. "So you like it?"

"If it fits, you need to get it. While you're doing that, I've got some clutches with my name on them."

On the eve of the ball, Arthur held open the door of his muscle car as she stepped out into the parking lot of the Shimmering Lake Country Club. "That dress looks stunning on you, darling."

Her heart fluttered. They kissed, he tossed his keys to the valet, and the night took off like a shot. They toured the crowds of people—men in uniforms and women in beautiful gowns. Arthur knew everyone in some capacity. His charm was a beacon. Small pockets of people eagerly awaited his arrival as they went from group to group. Finally, as the call to dinner was made, they sat at a table. She was flanked by Arthur and Cameron Gibbons. It was their first time meeting.

"Sit tight, babe." Arthur kissed her forehead. "I'm being summoned."

He rose from his chair and hurried over to a man at a podium flagging him down. Cameron took the opportunity to catch her attention and introduce himself.

"You must be Jerri? Arthur has told me all about you."

His voice was soft but eager. "I'm Cam. This is Amanda."

His date was pouring a clear liquid from a flask into a half-drunk cocktail.

"Yeah, hi. I'm Jerri," she said to both of them.

He told her about growing up in Smithville, a small rural town just a few miles away. She related to him with her tales about growing up in Montana.

"You're pretty young compared to most of these guys." She scanned the room, then looked back to Cam. "You've got the uniform on, and I'm pretty sure that's not a Scout getup," she said archly.

Cameron grinned and looked down at his medals. "Many of these guys were in and out of the military before I was born. I'm still navigating the "in" phase of military service. I'm a radar technician at a local Air Guard unit. This is my first time home since training."

"Air Guard?"

"It's like the community police version of the Air Force. I work on a local base. Get to go home and sleep in my own bed every night. It's nice."

"And how do you know Arthur?"

"He moved into town several years ago, and I met him while I was working. It was serendipitous, you know. He was a commando, like my dad. They even served together. Can you believe it?"

"Commando?" Jerri questioned.

Arthur took his seat to the right of Jerri, planting a strong kiss on her cheek.

"You guys talking about me?" he asked.

"Funny you should ask." Jerri chuckled.

"All good things, Arthur," Cameron said. "Mainly about you and my…"

A booming voice came over the loudspeakers. "Ladies and gentlemen, please take your seats. We are about to begin the ceremonies."

The speakers suddenly chirped with a high-frequency feedback loop, and the crowd cringed. The audio engineer, a slow, elderly veteran, quickly dropped the volume of the speakers.

"Darrel!" Arthur accosted him.

The ceremonies began with the pledge of allegiance, a flag ritual, and ended with a lengthy monologue by the guest of honor that began with an introduction about his upbringing in rural New Hampshire and ended with a diatribe about the enemies of our nation.

"He's full of hot air tonight," Arthur whispered to Jerri.

She slipped her hand into his. It was warm and calloused. It made her feel safe.

Throughout the night, he made her feel safe as they danced, held one another, and laughed. She felt like she was beginning to confide in him and to see his emotional capacity outside of the hard-nosed soldier he bragged about being.

At the end of the night, they closed the evening off with a joy ride in Arthur's new Corvette. He pressed the throttle down as they entered Interstate 146. The engine roared and pushed Jerri back into her seat. The highway was empty, and the moon was a glowing crescent against the blackness of the sky.

"So, what did you think?" Arthur asked as he pulled out a pack of cigarettes.

"I had an amazing time. Your friend Cameron is really nice," she said.

"He's a good kid. I'm glad he joined the Air Guard. His life is starting to come back together, you know?" He offered the pack of smokes to her.

"He told me you served with his dad. What was that like?" She asked as she pulled out a cigarette.

"Yeah. That was a long time ago."

He pulled out a smoke with his lips.

"Vietnam?"

"Yeah. I made a promise to Max, Cam's dad. I told him that if anything happened, I would look out for him."

"Arthur. That's incredible. You and Max must have been so close."

"Tricia, Cam's mom, she got into some trouble back in '80. So I came up here and watched over her. Made sure we kept the thugs at bay. That's what they call a Guardian Angel mission."

Once they ignited their smokes, he opened the moon roof and the wind rushed the cabin.

"Who calls it that?"

"Our team. I'm not supposed to reveal this information, but I never really left the Army. I'm protecting military secrets in Newport. There's a big naval station down there that needs our help. From time to time, we'll respond to domestic issues. Intercepting terror threats. I go up to Boston a lot for stuff. New York City or DC, occasionally."

"Wow. Is that what Cameron meant when he said commando?"

"That's a phrase we've used before, sure. They call us many things, but the thing I love the most is what our enemies call us."

Jerri looked at him, waiting for the word.

"Hunters."

He pushed the clutch in and dropped the transmission down a gear. The engine bellowed, and the tires struggled to grip the slick pavement. Arthur skillfully worked through the fishtail and touched Jerri's thigh. She moved his hand toward the opening of her skirt and parted her legs.

***

Jerri and Livvy watched a nurse adjust Arthur's bedding. He stepped out of the room and greeted them with a soft smile as he went past. Livvy entered first, slowly. Jerri watched her caution become fear as a forced exhale from a ventilation machine startled her. She moved in and wrapped her arm around Olivia's shoulder.

"It's okay, Livvy. It's to help your dad breathe." Jerri held her daughter as they stepped toward the bed.

Olivia swallowed hard. "Dad? Can you hear me?"

Steady chirps. Loud, mechanical exhales. His chest rose and fell, but his eyes stayed shut.

"Mom's here, too." She pulled a wad of tissues from her jacket pocket and wiped away her tears. "She brought some of your military stuff. I just… I don't understand. The pictures? You can't even open your emails. How did you learn to doctor photos in the '80s?"

When you had the kind of money your father had, you could buy any bullshit you wanted. And God, we bought bullshit, Jerri thought grimly.

"And what about my thirteenth, Dad? I—I don't know how I can ever forgive you for that," Olivia said. "You knew how important that was for Mom, and I told you how important it was for me. And it was like you took a page from Grandpa's playbook! You disappeared right when it mattered."

Jerri held her in a loving embrace and tried to soothe her.

"I remember, honey. It's okay. Everything's gonna be okay."

Olivia's wailing alerted the nurse, who found them holding one another over the intubated body. Another body that had become one with the hospital with its tubes, wires, and mechanisms. When they made eye contact, Jerri dismissed him and appreciated his distant empathy.

After some time, Livvy pulled away from her mother. "I'm going to the bathroom. I need to reload my tissues. There's snot all over me, isn't there?"

Jerri's face said enough.

"Great."

She watched Livvy exit, and turned back to her husband's body.

Digital chirps. The hissing and whirring of life-sustaining machinery.

She approached the bedside table where she had placed the shoe box and forms.

STATE HEALTH RECORDS—VETERAN'S DIVISION
FORM 1: SPOUSAL TERMINATION
ACKNOWLEDGMENT

She slid the shoe box cover off and pulled out a photo. It was Arthur and the Secretary of Defense. They smiled brightly at the camera. Arthur wore patterned military fatigues. He looked to be in his early twenties. She flicked the photo onto Arthur's chest.

"Fake." She whispered.

FORM 2: CREMATION VOUCHER FOR INDIGENTS

She retrieved another photo. Arthur stood with Max Gibbons, Cameron's father. They held compact rifles and wore similar uniforms and face paint. A jungle devoured the background behind them. Arthur could have paid to have those images doctored by a skilled software engineer in those days.

I knew you had money, but I didn't think you were using it for sick shit like this.

"Fake." She tossed the picture onto the first.

Her voice cracked. Hot tears streamed down her face.

FORM 3: MANDATORY ORGAN DONATION FORM

The next photo was her and Arthur at the Veteran's Day ball in 1987. She stared at it and seethed.

"I don't know what you did before you came up here and took advantage of me. And of Cam. And all of the saps that got in your way. You burned your bridges and fled. I get it. Tricia was an easy target. Then you met Cam and ruined his brain with lies. And then Olivia."

She scoffed.

"She's the one you lied to the least. Because you barely said anything to her. And when you did, it was fake. Just as fake as all of this is. I don't want to live like that anymore."

A heavy tear plopped down on the photo. She folded it in half and placed it in her purse.

FORM 4: END OF LIFE EXPENSES LOAN APPLICATION

"As far as the rest of these, you can have them. I'm sure they aren't worth anything, anyway."

She tucked the shoe box under the blankets next to Arthur's arm.

"This medical bill is going to fucking sink us, Art. Just to keep you alive for the next couple of days. And then they're pulling the plug. You have to wake up. You said you'd always take care of us. And now look at you, Art."

She balled her hands into tight fists.

"What were you thinking, not having any goddamn cash lying around? Or last wishes? Or a fucking safe somewhere. You must have something. Somewhere. Where is it? Wake up, Art! Wake up!"

"Mom?" Olivia asked.

Jerri spun around with her hand on her chest. "Sh— Livvy. How long have you been standing there?"

Olivia walked toward the bed and noticed the shoe box placed near Arthur. Her lip trembled as she placed a small, brown teddy bear between the blankets and the shoe box.

"Hey, folks. Sorry to bug you," the nurse said. "Visiting hours will be up in a few minutes."

The pair exited the hospital in silence. Hoary clouds slowly drifted in the illuminated sky. A bulbous full moon guided them.

"What do you think happens when you die?" Olivia asked.

"A lot of things, Livvy." Jerri replied and took a moment. She stared blankly through the windshield.

"Most of them happen right here. In the now. In a place where we can dance and feel and smell. When people go away, they have nothing to do with the now anymore. But I think they still exist, Livvy."

"I like that, Mom."

Crossroads

by
John Gillard

Crossroad

Confidently leaning into this space,
this space of overwhelming uncertainty.
Does my confidence hail from ignorance or a
connection to divinity?

Reflecting on the deeply rooted past, even though
it is nothing more than a reference, no longer an option.
Does the impossibility make it my preference?

Looking left, a seemingly short path
feeding my flesh, every sense on fire.
Is left the best choice because it feeds
every desire?

Glancing right, safe and purportedly predestined,
both taxing and rewarding. Either way I go, I
must proceed confidently.

The future holds an uncertain peace.
An inevitable lease on life, or death, such is the future.
Mind, heart, and soul open—removing all sutures neither
holding me together nor back. What is it that I lack?
Absolutely nothing.

The crossroad is a place of rest, where I left my last breath,
which influences but does not guarantee the next. The
crossroad is where I reside, as it exposes all, where
recovery begins right before the fall.
Either way, I'm here.

Spin cycle

A slight relief when the machine comes to its last cycle:
wash, rinse, spin until the need arises for us to do it all
again.

Branding is one of our greatest industries.
It requires some creativity but very little morality,
simply the capacity to spin reality.
The oppressed are conditioned to lean into a
manufactured boogeyman brand, while being asked
to forget systems of comprehensive lynching by those
who most benefit from this blatant sleight of hand.

An inhumane metamorphosis of sort, in reverse. Slavery
devolves into Jim Crow, mass incarceration fueled by the
delusion of supremacy and self-loathing, masking our
insecurities in labeled possessions, clothing—oh, and lies.

Caterpillars emerging from the cocoon instead of butterflies,
the spin.

Slavery is now human trafficking, where billionaires and
always complicit politicians polish turds, call them birds,
and somehow convince the masses they can fly.

When a judge coined the phrase "consensual rape,"
debatably because he saw more of himself in the rapist
than the victim, a scholar in our judicial system? We're
expected to trust him? We're expected to trust them?

I think we call it rebranding, pandering to profit so little
while losing so much. Completely out of touch.

We spend much of our energy consuming, as if we can
take it with us but there will come a time, as each of us draws
near to our last breath, where assuredly we will neither be
able to hold on to the fruits of our obsessive consumption,
nor rebrand, nor spin death.

Alarm rings, spin cycle ends.

Forgiveness

Forgetting the inhumanity,
offering love instead.

Remembering the insanity,
graciously feeding the unfed.

Intentionally loving those who hate.

Violently protecting the lives of loved ones,
even when they don't protect themselves.

Never conceding defeat,
especially not to the delusional elite.

Settling for nothing.

Seizing each opportunity to love someone or something.

The Blackest moment

The Blackest moment is less moment and more centuries.
It represents the darkness of the heart.

The human condition unchallenged yields strife. When
challenged it reveals the best of us.

The Blackest moment is merely a contrast to the light.

Lomie

She loves me and I love Lomie.
So special, so true.
The ability to make chaos homey.
She probably wouldn't like you.

Maya

She was neither perverted by formal education nor reliant on rules to mask insecurity, yet she taught at the highest level.

Spoke several languages, weathered many storms constantly fighting and defeating the devil in the form of trauma, sexism, racism and the rest.

She always gave her best, remaining comfortable with falling short, choosing to cultivate the life of, instead of abort, her dreams.

Few people leave an impact on this world like her. I miss her, her authenticity, and her purity. Her distinct voice, her righteous choice, the refusal to allow her trauma to force her into emotional obscurity.

I miss Maya.

Embrace

I do not give a ▮.
There are no ▮ to be given.
I hope you give a ▮.

Faith and fumes

When a man leaves war not all of him returns. Domestic or abroad, whether his enemies present themselves boldly or as the usual frauds—family, friends and acquaintances.

Men fight for everyone, distinction made between males and men, men bear the full weight of their responsibilities while males focus on props, presentation and social amenities. Let's begin again…

War never leaves men. There's no menstrual cycle to prep us to carry life, just broad shoulders and an affinity for supporting a wife, willingly forfeiting our life at any time to any random bump in the night.

By carrying the fight, it closes us off to receiving vital support. In fact, we often manufacture the battle at home, when we're workin,' and the worst part? The battle is obliviously being fought within.

Many of us don't know what questions to ask, content with wearing the "I'm FINE" mask. My friend would ask, "Do you know what FINE means? F***in Incapable of Normal Emotion!" and then we'd laugh.

It's no laughing matter as our chemistry predisposes us to aggression which demands self-awareness few of us possess, a combination hellbound on making a mess.

However, all is not lost as faith trumps all, the catalyst for change. The fuel to rearrange
our paths to peace, faith keeps us going when nothing else will, especially our will.

Although the fuel is reduced to fumes, it carries us through the battles, both within and without, allows us to smile instead of shout, denying our trauma a life in others, continuing to protect our sisters and brothers, not with the physicality of weapons, pushes, or shoves but the ultimate weapon…

The sharing of love.

Unk

Rough kid, pure heart, bright future, beyond humbling start but I love that moniker uncle, or "Unk," as some of my nieces and nephews exclaim.

Nieces and nephews of all ages, even great-, and great-great nieces and nephews. I love each and every one of them but honor a more active connection with few, such is life, not everyone sees you, nor you them.

They've protected my heart by allowing love to flow through a not-so-far removed bloodline, they have given so much just with their presence, the living legacy of my ancestors coming into focus despite the world's cruelest intent to choke us.

Choke the life and love right out of us, I digress, Unk not the unknown but the culmination of the near and distant existing in one space, I see my grandparents, parents and siblings in each little face. Amazing.

A simple conversation, the need to set boundaries, inside jokes, the Lord has truly blessed me to engage with these living legacies,

hearing them say, "I needed that Unk," or a simple, "I love you, too," the acknowledgment that your example, good and bad, has been of some use.

Those lost have been tragic, but I hold their beauty close to the living, the fond memories, a cooing baby girl with a small scar on her head, three brilliant boys taken far too soon, and a beautiful young lady who could only attach to the pain before letting go. All angels, this I know.

The near and far, coexisting in the same spaces, I see the purest love in each and every one of their faces.

… just call me Unk.

Almost bare

An almost bare tree, remnants of a canvas once offering lush green leaves, fresh air through several seasons, providing covering, stimulating for so many reasons.

An almost bare tree, yellowing leaves scattered along the road. Once vibrant, rich as it complimented life. Now requiring clean up. Happens slowly yet feels so abrupt.

An almost bare tree, dependent upon the season it could be representative of you, or me, an almost bare tree.

Black Veteran

At least three generations of fighting for the double victory.

Let's speak the unspoken to ensure there's no mystery, none of the double speak of celebrating diversity, equity and inclusion, which at its very core is a downright lie.

I would be remiss to call it an illusion or even a delusion, the deeply rooted intent has existed from the inception of our great but horribly flawed country.

Racism is not lessened by our service, no matter how stellar our performance,
regardless of the policy we cannot legislate the human heart, yet another false start.

But all hope is not lost, but hope deferred comes with a cost like unfulfilled potential, we ask, "What could have been?" But with hope we ask, "What will be, if we open our hearts and see, genuinely, authentically without a self-serving agenda?"

One of the many answers to this question is illustrated, despite being unplanned.

This hope is embodied by the Black Veteran

No overblown cultural pride, everything in moderation, the self-loathing carried over from the accepted inferiority propaganda has compromised our unity, fractured our community.

Black Veteran, we've proudly fought for our country now we must fight for ourselves, fight for the wealth borne from generations of service, even if it was introduced under duress,

continue to fight for each blessed breath.

Black Veteran.

Standing watch

No light pollution in the middle of the desert, downpouring rain

Conducting a roving watch, ensuring the rest could sleep safely

I never forgot how drenched I was, the hardest rainfall I've ever experienced

There was no shelter to which I could retreat, the rain rendered my waterproof gear useless

From that day forth, I appreciated the ability to seek refuge, but not without savoring the rain, if not only but for a few extra moments

Today, I sit in the rain alone watching children master their body awareness in sport, quietly offering support

A few looks from others, as if to say, "why are you sitting in the rain? Alone?"

My heart quietly answers this imagined inquiry, with a simple, defenseless "I'm healing and thankfully never alone."

Enshrinement

Worshipping the dead
while neglecting the living.
Oblivious souls
taking, clueless to giving.
Miserable existence.

'ship has sailed

Will it end the way it began,
full of passion and desire?
Comfort dictates our inevitable fate,
Either reinvigorate or expire.

Primal, intuitively feeding and receiving a sustenance that
inspires,
Once the novelty has waned, what will become of us? Will
it be too late?
Will it end the way it began,
full of passion and desire?

Will it die, like so many others?
Placed on a shelf, deprioritized, void of the initial fire?
Either reinvigorate or expire.

We tried but trust was lost, our hearts and commitment
began to tire,
Longing and pulling away, there's so much at stake!
Will it end the way it began,
full of passion and desire?

Is it an opportunity for growth,
or have we been too badly burned from the now grueling
fire?
I know, it's too late.
Either reinvigorate or expire.

Holding out hope, emotionally it's coming down to the wire,

Staying must be sincere, can't be faked.
Will it end the way it began,
full of passion and desire?
Either reinvigorate or expire.

For those in the spiritual nosebleed seats

Futilely attempting to find safety in culture, either their own or others

Deathly afraid of humility, neither aware, nor connected, you neither accept nor respect it

what's in the mirror, what the hell do you know about the universe, how odd? Truth be told, you really don't even give a damn.

Overfilled with pride, ineffectively trying to hide. Culture never was nor will it ever be God, therefore I will only worship I AM.

Burned

Undeniably,
The fire was brightly ablaze.
Do you remember?
The loud crackling did amaze.
Reduced to smoke and embers.

Codependent dissonants

We confuse irreverence
with courage, honesty, and candor.

Nothing more than base.

We don't think twice about disregarding anything of
relevance,
reduced to cold porridge, a travesty or a plain old bore.

Then we need space, either when discussing race or when
we're encouraged to stand on anything, more specifically
our faith.

Oh, but while many claim to be Christians, we know very
little of Christ.

Demanding a stance on character and faith is a quick way to
witness men turn to mice, warm hearts to ice.

We can all agree the crucifixion was horrible, a torture
beyond average.

Sadly, in our socially evolved era, we'd do it all over again,
only difference we'd be considerably more savage.

But we love politics, we adore the dissonance between
thoughts and actions, breaking down into powerful yet
morally corrupt factions.

Liberals, conservatives, independents—all carnivores, shameless attention whores.

What do we really know about independence?

Nothing more than a collective of cowardly dissonant codependents.

GRa.i.VE

by
Patrick Lachey

Amidst the tumultuous chaos, the contracted security detail desperately seeks refuge in the ARTEMIS housing bunker, a fortress of secrets hidden deep within the rocky, desolate terrain. Dim emergency lighting casts eerie, flickering shadows across cold, concrete walls, and the suffocating scent of dust and fear hangs in the air.

Alex's ears still ring from the deafening blast, and his vision blurs as he stumbles forward. Lieutenant Dimitri pulls him to his feet, his face etched with fear, determination, and unspoken camaraderie. The troops' footfalls echo with urgency as they sprint through dimly lit corridors, their breaths ragged.

The frenzied battle rages around them. Bullets spark and ricochet off metal surfaces, and explosions light up the subterranean maze in orange hues. The winding passages seem endless, each one a potential deathtrap. Sweat soaks Alex's brow and his heart pounds as they press forward. The attackers are unyielding, their numbers overwhelming, and their intentions absolute. It is a relentless struggle against an inexorable adversary. A voice on the coms cuts through the cacophony of warfare, its tone urgent and strained.

"Alex, you need to hurry," it pleads. "There isn't much time. A large convoy of troops is barreling toward your location."

Alex clenches his jaw. "I know! But you better ready the contingency just in case."

The voice wavers. A surge of static crackles through the radio.

"I don't want to make that call with you still there. You have to hurry."

"I'm working on it. Now stop squawking in my ear so I can start making some goddamn progress," Alex says as he directs Lieutenant Dimitri's team to press forward.

Dimitri and his men continue their advance, Alex in tow. Hallways hiding small, fortified machine gun nests and wall-mounted guns harry them at every turn. The team razes the traps like a volcano pouring liquid death, pelting the enemy with a continuous assault of EMP blasts to subdue the targeting capabilities of the cannons, and pounding each hallway like a sledgehammer to a walnut. Blood and smoke fill their wake as they reach the inner sanctum of the facility.

Alex approaches the device housing the elusive A.I. ARTEMIS. His heart races as he finally lays eyes on the thing that has overwhelmed his life for the last few months, his blind sense of purpose finally within his grasp. His fingers tremble as he initiates the retrieval process. The seconds tick away mercilessly. Approaching footsteps echo in the distance and the voice on the coms interrupts his concentration.

"Alex, you have to get out of there," it urges.

"I really would have thought as a military man, Dad, you would have better radio etiquette," Alex says as he types feverishly.

"Now isn't the time for jokes, Alex. You shouldn't even be there in the first place," his father's voice crackles through the radio.

Time is slipping through their fingers like sand in an hourglass and the world's fate hangs in the balance. Each keystroke, each passing moment, carries the weight of the world's destiny as Alex races against the impending storm of destruction.

"What is this? The code doesn't make any sense. The variables are all wrong and it doesn't seem to align with—"

A piercing shrill blasts through the coms and Alex swats his earpiece out of his ear.

"What the fuck? These coms are supposed to be secured; interference shouldn't be possible with the satellite overlay."

The buzz of static wasps rises again.

"Al—are… *shhh* there?"

Alex reinserts his earpiece with a wince. "Yeah, I'm here."

"Imaging shows two additional forces inbound. You need to move your team to the upper level for extraction. Do you have the device?"

"I have it, but something feels off. The code looks like it was written by a child, and the locking mechanisms were already open. Are our coms being scrambled? I'm hearing some interference." Alex waves Lieutenant Dimitri and his team to the stairwell.

"We haven't heard anything unusual, and all channels are open and clear. What is the update on your location?"

"We're making our ascent up the southern stairwell. Should lead us to the cargo hold."

A deafening shriek sounds from the earpiece. Alex tears the headset off completely and stops as the team enters the cargo hold. The hold is scattered with Conex boxes and a few vehicles. Flickering lights along the wall lead to a large cargo bay door. The bay seems different from the rest of the facility. There is no security, no wall-mounted cannons. Not an ounce of resistance anywhere when just moments before they had been fighting for their lives.

The team rushes to open the cargo bay door and Alex grabs his computer to run diagnostics on the module. Code streams across Alex's screen and it doesn't make any fucking sense. Bright light pierces the hold as Lieutenant Dimitri's team opens the bay door. Alex turns away and closes his computer. Time to go.

They rush outside to an expanse of nothing. No vehicles, no troops, no extraction team, nothing. Alex puts the headset back on and calls on Coms.

"We're outside, do you copy?"

No answer.

"Lieutenant Dimitri! My coms are down, are you getting a response?"

No answer.

Alex walks towards Dimitri. "Hello? Lieutenant? Do you have coms?"

The lieutenant doesn't move. He is as still as the dead air. Alex grabs Dimitri's shoulder to turn him around.

He has no face. Alex jerks his hand away. All of the members of the team are poorly rendered faceless things.

"What the fuck?"

Alex whirls around, taking in everyone with him: their lifeless bodies upright, faces flat panes with weird symbols streaming over and over like badly written code.

The earpiece crackles with static and the slight whisper of a woman's voice edges through.

*"Shhhhhhhhhhhhhhhhhh…*I.tried…*shhhhhh…*not enough time….*shhhhhhhhh."*

Alex stiffens. That nagging familiarity settles into place like a mechanical key switch.

"Well fuck, I guess there is no getting around it now, is there?"

Alex walks to the center of the group, digs through Dimitri's bag, and pulls out two grenades.

"Your code is terrible, coms are trash, and the detail in the final layers of the program was lacking. You almost had me, but in hindsight, I truly expected more.

Alex cups the headset microphone to his mouth and whispers, "Thank you."

Static in his earpiece crackles faintly.

"Now, smile for the camera and wait for the flash!" Alex releases his fingers and two safety levers fly off.

"Cheese!"

<SIMULATION TERMINATED, PROGRAM RUN ERROR>

Consoles light the dark space as researchers stare at the massive monitor in silence. The space contains large computer terminals and link stations utilized for deep diving into cyber and augmented reality space. Code can be built here from within to enhance the security features and allow for maximum control of even the most complicated programs. Only one of the four links is occupied. The terminal lights up and disengages as a man removes his headset and sits up from the metallic chair hugged by keyboards and monitors.

"God dammit, how did he figure it out? Those nodes and safeties this run took an eternity to build and he saw right through it! Who oversaw the safety blocks? I want a full report before we attempt to go back in."

"You can't possibly think another attempt will be authorized soon, Colonel?" a slender woman says as she secures the flashing error message and brings life to the room again. She yells commands to reset the program and sends technicians to the colonel's link station for diagnostics.

"Yes Arley, I do plan to go back in as soon as I can," the colonel says, clenching his fists.

Arley adjusts her glasses. "Yes, Colonel Darnix, right away." She secures power to the link station for system updates. When she is finished, the colonel joins her at the console. "Arley, walk with me." They walk down a long corridor lined with lights. Small robots skitter to and fro as they maintain the glossy sheen of the tiled floors. The Nexus-1 was a state-of-the-art research and development center for the Department of Defense that also acted as the central hub for all cyber, virtual, and augmented reality missions. The evolution of society and conflict paved the way for different types of war. Ground troops were rarely needed unless certain low-tech cells in underdeveloped countries started to cause trouble.

They stop at a large glass window looking into a room at the end of the hallway.

"He seems to be getting better at evading our access," the colonel says. "Maybe the scenario needs to be changed. Do we have other variants that we can run where he wouldn't know we're trying to access the programs?"

"You and I both know how he can evade and detect," Arley says. "He was always exceptional when it came to cyber mapping and coding. He was top of his class for a reason. With that, every time we run a different scenario from the one he just collapsed, he catches on much faster because we are essentially using his memories. This scenario is different because it's his most recent memory, so it's easier to control and manage. Despite him terminating this last run it is still our best option for a scenario."

Arley can't help but look at her father as he stares into the room. The conflict that had been gnawing at her for a long time nearly consumes her. She hesitates before speaking in a hushed voice. "Father, we need to talk about Alex like he's still Alex."

Colonel Darnix glances at her, his eyes heavy with the weight of their shared secret. "Arley, not now," he whispers, his voice barely audible over the hum of the machines in the next room.

Arley persists. "No, it's been too long. Alex is my brother, your son. He's only stuck in this situation because of a terrible decision *you* made to bomb the facility just as he fully integrated into ARTEMIS."

"Keep your voice down," Colonel Darnix says through clenched teeth. "You know why I had to do it, Arley. The A.I. was becoming too powerful, too unpredictable. It posed a significant threat to our national security. I had to make that difficult decision to protect our country."

Arley's eyes well up with tears. "Alex is trapped in this virtual prison because of you. I was there, I saw it happen, and I know why Alex did what he did. I also know if the roles were reversed he would not have done what you did."

The colonel closes his eyes and lets out an exasperated sigh. "You're probably right. Alex was special in how he always seemed to know just how to handle any situation. He was a lot like your mother in that regard." He rests his hand on Arley's shoulder. "I will bring him back even if I have to use LC-7 to do it."

The words land like a slap and Arley jerks back.

"You can't be serious!?" She winces and lowers her voice. "Father, why would you use that? It's dangerous. It has caused so much heartache."

The colonel turns his back to her, unable to hold her gaze. "I know it is and it has already taken so much from us. However, it got your brother into this mess, so maybe it will get him out." He walks down the hall and pauses only a moment to speak over his shoulder. "I already lost your mother. I will not lose Alex, too. No matter the cost, I will get him back."

Arley returns to the window and puts her hand on the glass "No matter the cost?" On the other side of the glass stand two identical link stations modified with life support systems. This space is used for people injured during cyber dives that result in trauma, who need recovery from the cyber overload triggered by extreme stress while fully integrated.

"I will bring you home, Alex." She drops her hand from the glass between her and her brother's comatose body and walks away.

"My research is almost complete. The final tests will be later this afternoon. Once they are successful, we'll probably go down in the history books, as Alex would put it," Chief Researcher Lydia Darnix says. "I'll send over the data before the day is out, unless you'll be here for the testing."

"As much as I would love to be there, I can't be in two places at once. I need to submit last month's research and give my seminar tonight. Besides, Dad and our golden boy will be there with you, so it will be fine."

Lydia laughs.

"Arley, stop calling your brother that. I suppose I can't keep mothering you forever, can I? Good luck tonight with your event. I love you and look forward to the next time you're at the lab."

"Love you too, Mom. And tell Dad I'll be there for his promotion next week; I feel we've all been so busy lately. I gotta run though, talk more soon."

Call ended flashes on the screen and Lydia walks back to the lab. As the doors open, a young man runs up to her.

"Hey Mom!"

Lydia jolts back, hand to her chest. "Jesus Christ Alex, you scared me half to death. Why on earth are you here so early?"

"Oops, didn't mean to startle you like that, just got a little excited is all. I made some adjustments I wanted to run by you before we go into testing this afternoon," Alex says as the displays in the room turn on.

"I managed to increase output and throughput with the surgical implants used for regulating the nanomachines." Alex starts typing on the nearby console.

"It will increase the safeties already installed, allowing us to regulate the instability of the machines, and it will increase control over deeper dives. This will allow for less impact on the brain which in turn reduces the high index for the failsafe to engage."

The lab's monitors fill the room with images of a brain, calculations, and parameter windows.

"I've already made the changes and dove twice, so I can account for my math. These changes will improve and…" Alex's words dry up as he takes in the shock on his mother's face.

"Umm, did I do something wrong?"

"Alex, how did you calculate this so fast? We just did a trial run last night in preparation for today," Lydia says as she reviews the images on the screen.

"Oh, I uhh, may have stayed up all last night since it was bothering me. The threshold for the failsafe seemed higher than it needed to be, so I umm… fixed it, I guess." he grins.

"Alex, I have to start off with how incredibly impressed I am with these changes, especially in the time you had to make them and then follow-up test. However, you won't be able to participate in today's trials."

Alex runs to his mother, a little frazzled. "Wait, why can't I be in the trial? I figured my changes would make me the ideal candidate since I was the candidate for the previous baseline anyway."

"Well, last night after running through the final trials, I sent over the data which your sister dropped off for review. The layouts, data points, parameters, and full summary were included. If we proceed with the trial today and the Board sees your parameters are different from the trial report, they'll realize you made these changes without the authorization or supervision of the lab's Chief Researcher. Which was incredibly irresponsible, by the way." Lydia crosses her arms. "You're now considered overclocked in your abilities, and in order for you to run this trial with your new baseline, I would be forced to reschedule the trials with the Board. Which in turn would force your father to delay his program just before his upcoming promotion ceremony."

"Riiiight. Damn, Mom, I'm sorry. I got so excited I didn't think of the ramifications on today's trials." Alex's hands tighten, and he lowers his head.

"It's fine, Alex, don't fret. Since our blockers were the same parameters last night, I'll run the trial and you will present to the Board," Lydia says with a smirk.

Alex perks up and lets out an exasperated sigh. "Ugh, well I had that coming, I guess. I'll go and prepare. Oh! Before I go, I came up with a name for the project. I think you'll find it fitting." Alex passes a piece of folded paper to his mother.

Lydia opens it and looks at her son with a droll expression. "Seriously?"

"Absolutely." He walks out of the lab chuckling. The doors open before he hits the button, and Alex nearly walks face first into his father.

"What the fu—oh! Sorry Dad, I'll be more careful," Alex says with his signature grin and skirts around his father as he leaves.

"What was that all about?" asks Lieutenant Colonel Darnix as he makes his way to Lydia.

"Oh James, it's just Alex being Alex, really." Lydia leans in for a kiss from her husband. "He managed to overclock his blocker in such a way that he is able to process information at a nearly superhuman level *and* have better control over the machine. He also did all of this overnight with full tests to back up his modifications."

"Well he sure didn't get that from me," says James. "That is definitely all you right there."

"Yeah, I know. Daddy has his little girl and Mommy her little boy, I guess." Lydia sighs and rubs her temples. "There will be a slight change in today's trial. Since our "golden boy" as Arley puts it, decided to go way above and beyond, I will be in the trial today for the Board's demonstration while Alex presents. And, your son decided to name the program." Lydia hands the folded paper to James.

"Lydi-CANE 7." James laughs. "Okay, maybe there is some of me in there after all. How about for today we just refer to it as LC-7 and circle back to it?"

"Fine by me," Lydia says as they laugh.

The afternoon arrives and Lieutenant Colonel Darnix walks the board members into the lab for the presentation and trial demonstrations. He is greeted by Alex, who is not his usual grinning self. He nods to his father and shakes the hands of the board members, then directs them to take their seats.

"Fellow members of the Board, thank you for joining us today for the demonstration of the LydiC—" He catches himself mid-word at his father's displeased look. "I mean the LC-7 project." The lieutenant colonel nods.

"Today you will witness the culmination of Chief Researcher Lydia Darnix's last seven years of work. This project will allow multiple interfaces per user and allow higher safety measures for a single user to do the work of a whole team at the same speed, if not faster."

Alex enters a few commands in the terminal in front of him and monitors light up with information while a massive steel shutter opens to a viewing panel of the next room.

"Now, as the data we provided to you states, the surgically implanted blockers allow the users to control the Cyberspace Augmented Nano Enhancer machines, or CANE for short, and prevent them from becoming unstable." Images of the implant appear on the screens for the Board to view and the amplification data follows. "Doing so allows for the CANE to monitor the user's vitals, repair damage in an instant, and allow the brain to essentially overclock mental abilities and take on a more strenuous workload. "Chief Darnix will be running the trial on the other side of this sealed room." Alex directs the attention to the window.

Lydia steps forward. "Good afternoon members of the board, and thank you, Alex, for your help getting to this point. As you can see here, I have six control consoles which I will simultaneously dive into and extract data from to demonstrate how the system works. Normally, a single link takes the participation of a small team supporting the user directly interfacing. I will utilize six links with only the help of the LC-7," Lydia takes a seat inside the link station, then takes an injector to her neck and administers the LC-7.

"Let us begin then, shall we?"

The room's lights dim and the trial begins. Alex and his father take a seat next to the monitoring station. Six display units show a faint glow as bursts of information appear on the screens for the Board to see. Data flows like a torrential flood, massive data spikes seamlessly navigated by a single individual. One monitor shows a nexus of data being compiled while another display shows aerial diagnostics of various satellites above Earth. The board members murmur amongst themselves in low, impressed tones. A few of them shake hands and nod at each other. James leans over to his son to check the monitors.

A look of horror grows on his son's face.

"Alex, what is wrong?"

"Look at this data spike on Mom's vitals. Something is attacking the system at an incredible rate and the LC-7 is having a hard time handling it. Whatever this is, it's processing information unlike anything I've ever seen." Alex tears away from the monitor and runs to another console. "We have to get Mom out of there or she could die!"

The lights in the lab flash red and the warning sirens of a cyber attack blink across the monitors.

A security team arrives inside the lab to escort the board members to a safe location as Alex types feverishly in an attempt to safely extract his mother.

"Alex, the door, hurry!"

The door securities bypass with a ping and slide open. James runs into the room as Lydia's body flails and the security straps tear free. Protrusions of LC-7 jet from her body in a glittering mist of blood and metal.

"Alex, what's happening?" shouts James. He stumbles to the ground as the protrusions sprout into silvery tendrils that whip through the air.

"Dad, you have to get out of there. Mom's blocker isn't responding and the nanomachines are running unchecked. The fail-safes are not registering. I can't shut it down!" Alex lunges at another console and slams out commands on the workstation.

James pushes to his feet, and the straps on the link station fly free. He faces an abomination of tendrils and jets of shrapnel surrounding the body of his wife. "Lydia, I'm so sorry."

A savage lash of tendrils flings James away and the nightmare of nanomachines and flesh stalks toward the door.

"Dad, get out of there now! We have to contain this. If LC-7 is left unchecked it could absorb this facility. I have to seal the room."

James lunges to his feet, runs to the blast door, and dives out. With a click and a command from Alex's console, the doors snap shut. James crawls to the observation window. The horror that was once his wife, now a mechanical monster, attacks the door. James bangs on the glass and shouts for his wife's attention.

Lydia stops and spins, then rushes the window. Tendrils warp into mechanical blades that pelt the glass like hail. Strikes veer left and right, coating the glass in a spider web of scratches as it struggles to break through the panel.

James, sweating, heart pounding in his throat, turns to his son Alex. "Alex, what can we do?" His voice is raspy and panicked.

"I don't know what this is and I'm trying to contain it!" Alex screams as he enters a final key prompt on the center workstation before dashing off to the emergency control panel.

He grows still.

"Dad, I have to scrub the room." He poises his hand over a red button. Tears stream down his cheeks.

"No, you can't. Your mother, we can't do this to her!"

James turns back to the window. The nightmarish abomination void of any similarity to his wife strikes at the glass and it cracks.

James places his hand on the glass. "I'm so sorry Lydia."

He jerks his hand back as the emergency shutter closes and locks into place. James stares at his son.

Alex stands, trembling, with his hands depressed over the button.

The speakers announce, *Emergency scrubbing protocol activated.*

The crackle of static charges and explosions of intense heat fill the room. Relentless pounding rattles the shutter doors as a dull orange glow seeps through the seams and the smell of hot metal fills the air. James stares blankly at the mechanical shutter where his wife last smiled at him.

Biological signatures: negative. Cybernetic signatures: negative. Electrical pulses: negative. Emergency scrub complete.

The doors and shutter open to the room. There is nothing left but charred panels on the walls and a melted link station in the center of the room.

Alex is back at the console working without a second glance. James walks toward him. "Alex, what are you doing?"

One of Alex's monitors displays *download completed* while another says *aerial satellite imaging received, location found.*

"Alex, what is this?"

Alex walks to another console and grabs a data drive out of the computer.

"Alex! Talk to me, what are you doing?" Alex ignores his father and walks back to the center console confirming the aerial imaging location. "I found you," he whispers.

James runs to his son and grabs him by the shoulder, spinning him around. "Alex, what is going on? What are you doing?"

There is a fire behind Alex's red-rimmed eyes. He pushes his father's hand off his shoulder. "I'm going after the people who made me kill my mother," he says through gritted teeth. Alex pulls away from his father and powers down the monitors in the room, then storms out of the lab.

***

The colonel awakens covered in sweat and clamps both hands on his temples. He walks to his washroom, splashes water on his face and towels off, then stares at his reflection. He sees the face of a man that once had the entire world, filled with joy and happiness, now a broken shell struggling to keep it together. He looks over at his console. There are nine missed calls from the Board's conference room. He meets his gaze in the mirror, throws the towel on the counter, and walks out of his room.

***

Arley brews a kettle of tea, slices a lemon, and then walks back to her desk. As she sits, she replays the footage of the day they lost their mother. She jots down notes, rewatching certain parts, focusing on the interactions between her father and brother. She loads up the observation room video and plays them next to each other, lining up the time stamps.

Father gets pushed away, tossed like a ragdoll. She filters out noise, enhances verbal sounds, and silences the alarms. She focuses on her father.

"Lydia, I'm so sorry"

Rewind

"Lydia, I'm so sorry"

Rewind

"Lydia, I'm so sorry"

Arley writes in her notebook. She moves to Alex's footage and notices that a download has started on one of the monitors near Alex. She focuses on Alex's face, filters out sounds, and hears nothing but typing on the console. Arley rewinds a little further and sees Alex dash over to the computer and plug in a drive before he goes back to the center console where the download starts on the monitor. She notes the timestamps. The phone rings.

Arley sits up and drops her pen. She answers the call.

"Hello?"

"Arley, I need you to prep the LC-7 and the other link station in the med bay."

She hesitates, silence hanging on both ends of the call. Arley finally speaks.

"Yes, sir. I can have it ready in under an hour. Which scenario will we be running for this event?"

Her father sighs, and there's so much exhaustion in the sound.

"We will run the actual event, no modifications."

Arley squeezes the phone. "Are you sure?"

"Yes, I'm sure. I will be going in to meet him directly. No more scenarios will be needed. I'll meet you in the medical bay." The call ends.

Arley stands up and closes her computer, tucks her notebook in her research coat, and grabs her cup of tea. As she heads to the door, her computer pings. But her computer is off.

She returns to her desk. When she opens the screen, her grip goes light with shock and her cup crashes to the floor.

***

The colonel arrives in the medical bay and begins preparations on his link station, then changes into a dive suit. As he clasps the final strap into place, Arley walks in. Her expression is tight as she stares at her father and then at Alex's body on the opposite table. She approaches with a small case and lays it down next to her father. James looks at his not-so-little girl anymore, who carries so much weight on her shoulders, always.

"Arley, everything will be fine. We have updated the safeties since the last time and the room is installed with the emergency fittings. This room is also equipped with all of the life-saving systems needed once he returns. I know you're worried, but we don't have any other choices left."

Arley brushes the hair from her face and adjusts her glasses. "I know it will be fine. Once Alex is back, he'll make it better. That golden boy always did. I always gave Mom a hard time, but I hope she knew that I was only joking. Alex is very special. I'll be happy to have him back." She unlocks the small case and hands her father an injector.

"Mom's overprotectiveness seems to be wearing off on me. This injector contains the LC-7. Just before we commence the dive sequence, you'll inject it and the blocker will…" Arley cuts off as tears form in her eyes.

The colonel's expression gentles. "Arley, what's wrong?"

"My apologies, Sir. The memories from last time just sort of caught up to me, and maybe I'm overtired." Arley wipes her cheek.

James rests his hand on Arley's shoulder. "It's ok. I know what to do and I know the dangers. Since Alex and ARTEMIS are essentially one, we don't risk an attack like last time. Alex made sure of that. I will bring your brother back." James returns to the link station to finalize preparations.

Arley follows her father and kisses him on the cheek. On her way out she stops at the doorway and glances up at the cameras, then turns back and leaves the room.

The lab falls into a deeper silence. The researchers know that failure isn't an option, and they're determined to leave no room for error. Tension and anxiety punctuates every movement as the team finalizes preparations.

Arley stands at her console, unwavering.

"Let us begin. Administer the LC-7 and proceed with the dive."

A monitor in the lab shows Colonel Darnix injecting the dark vial into his neck.

"I want vitals on my screen of both participants and a full update on any parameter shifts of the same, regardless of whether they are in acceptable zones."

<SIMULATION START, ACCESS GRANTED, CHANNELS OPEN>

Dimitri and his men continue their advance, Alex in tow. Hallways hiding small, fortified machine gun nests and wall-mounted guns harry them at every turn. The team razes the traps like a volcano pouring liquid death, pelting the enemy with a continuous assault of EMP blasts to subdue the targeting capabilities of the cannons and pounding each hallway like a sledgehammer to a walnut. Blood and smoke fill their wake as they reach the inner sanctum of the facility.

"Hello, Alex."

The colonel stands in the center of the room. He waves his hand and Dimitri and the security detail vanish. The lights in the once dark room shine like daylight. Colonel Darnix walks over to his son. Alex just stares.

"What's wrong? Are you not happy to see me? I mean you must be a little surprised at the very least."

Alex cracks his classic smile and lets out a laugh.

"Yes Dad, I am happy to see you. I was getting tired of all these simulations and essentially reliving the best and worst moments of my life on loop while my physical body lies next to you, lifeless as we speak, yeah?"

The colonel's eyes widen. "Uh, yes it is, but how did you know that?"

"Because I can see it. You don't bond with the world's strongest A.I. and not pick up a few perks." Alex blinks away and appears behind his father. "I also knew that this was the simulation you would choose to run since it was my last 'physical memory.'" Alex air quotes with a smile. "It allows you to run it over and over again with a higher success rate since my brain was not fully able to process it before you decided to blow up the facility and bury me."

"Alex, after we saw what you did to those men I had no choice. Once you connected to ARTEMIS you took control of the mainframe of the lab and started massacring everyone. I wasn't sure if it was you or the machine any longer, so I made a decision." James spun to face Alex, but he blinked away to another part of the room.

"Sad part is, Father, you did know I was in control. Did I get a little carried away? Yeah definitely. Can you blame me? I found the device that triggered Mom's blocker to stop working, which caused LC-7 to be set free, run amok, and force me to kill her." Alex blinks closer and closer to James, stopping a few paces away.

James stumbles backward, righting himself at the last moment.

"What you heard from Mom before the demonstration was that I had overclocked my implants and had run tests. But how do you think I managed to prove my data?"

"Because you were already using LC-7," says James as he clenches his fists then lunges forward to swing at Alex.

Alex blinks away.

"Because I was already using LC-7, that's right. Something you figured out after I had touched ARTEMIS and bonded with it. You used Mom's data that we sent over and tuned ARTEMIS to attack. I will forgive the fact that there is a chance you had absolutely no idea the effect it would have, however, you also didn't seem to think about the user. Mom had to go in place of me because she thought running the test with my new enhancements would have been a false positive to her life's work. I'm mad at you, but

I feel based on your missed call log the Board was hoping this was *done and done* so it couldn't be traced back to them and you could start weaponizing this tech. They seem to be very mad this isn't handled yet."

Arley stands up from her workstation after watching this conversation unfold on the monitor, then locks the blast doors behind her.

"Alex, you're talking nonsense. I would never do anything to endanger you or your mother."

"Dad, chill. I didn't see it at first. It wasn't till Mom saw the data after you bombed the lab trying to seal me and your dark secret away." Alex appears back in front of James.

The shock becomes fury on James's face. "What?! What are you talking about Alex? Your mother is dead. My wife is dead!" James lunges for Alex again, and again he flickers just out of reach.

"Mom's physical body is gone, but her subconscious is still here. When I realized I couldn't contain the anomaly, I downloaded her consciousness to a drive. It was the best I could do."

"Hello, James."

James's breath catches at the voice and all the red anger drains from his face as he turns toward the voice.

"Oh my God, Lydia? Is that really you?"

Lydia blinks from view and appears next to Alex.

"Oh James, how could you?"

James collapses in a heap on his knees. "The Board needed testing done for another project. They had planned on using your work and ARTEMIS to make cyber soldiers.

The promotion was riding on it, Lydia. Think of what we could have accomplished with better funding, better clearance, better everything. ARTEMIS was supposed to integrate that day and copy the coding for LC-7, nothing more."

Alex and Lydia flash in front of James. Alex paces his hand on James's head and his father screams in pain.

In the medical bay, the colonel's vitals spike and his blocker deactivates.

"What have you done? How am I able to feel pain here?" Sweat slicks his brow and spittle flies between his gritted teeth.

"It's simple actually. You were using LC-7, which is no longer protecting you, but attacking you. With your blocker deactivated you are fully susceptible to the stressors of this simulation," Alex says, walking away from his writhing father.

***

The medical bay doors close as red emergency lights flash. Nanomachines pour out of the colonel.

***

"Please, don't do this. I don't want to die," pleads James as he struggles to fight through the pain and stand up.

"I'm not going to kill you Dad, I'm not you. You can stay here and catch up with Mom. I'm sure you can spend however long you need to find the words to tell her you're sorry."

The room goes white closes in around the colonel. As it condenses into a transparent sphere, Lydia and Alex flicker out of the glassy prison. They stare at the colonel with his face pressed against the wall of the sphere.

"Alex! Let me out of here! I'm sorry! Let me out of here!" As James watches his family disappear, tears stream down his face and he collapses from the pain again. With a final whimper he whispers, "let me out."

***

Back in the medical bay, the colonel's body erupts with tendrils that lash and bind themselves to the life support equipment in the room. The machines grow and absorb the link station, then spill onto the floor and creep towards Alex's body. The colonel's head explodes in a web of striking blades. Lights in the room flicker then burst to dust as the biomechanical abomination continues to absorb material and grow.

The Nexus-1 goes on full emergency lockdown and evacuation protocol is initiated. The hallways flood with panicked personnel while security tries to maintain order and evacuate. The researchers in the primary lab start to scream as they realize the shutter doors won't open and they're trapped inside. EMERGENCY CONTAINMENT PROTOCOL appears on the main monitor of the lab. They watch in horror as the medical bay images display on the screen. What is left of the colonel, scrapes and claws at the doors and windows.

Arley stands outside of the medical bay and watches as Alex's body is consumed by the mass. She slides an emergency control key into a panel and hovers over the red button. She rests her hand on the window and fixes her gaze on the camera just before the nanomachines smash it to powder.

She pushes the button.

The blast doors slam shut to the sound of explosions and the hum of electricity as the emergency scrub program purges the room. Arley tucks the key in her pocket and walks out of the facility with the rest of the evacuees.

***

Two days later, the Nexus-1 is on lockdown and the fires are finally under control. Security surrounds the perimeter. A burnt husk is all that remains of the state-of-the-art facility. Smoke and the scent of scorched metal and concrete linger in the hallways. Emergency lights still flash and ventilation cycles out smoke and fumes as best it can on limited reserve power. The main hub of the Nexus-1 is a tomb of the burnt skeletal remains of the research team collecting data for the Board in secret to create their weapon out of Lydia's work.

Further down the hallway is the medical bay. The blast doors open and behind the glass is a spider-webbed mass of dead machines. The room begins to shake and a partially absorbed EKG registers a faint heartbeat on Alex's table. As the monitor pings louder and stronger, the mass of dead machines crumble and flake off to the floor.

An amorphous blob of living machines seeps out of the cracking cocoon of dead hardware. A faint glow trickles into the room as the vibrations of the moving mass generate light, speckling the room like a disco ball. The remaining shell crumbles away, revealing a crouched figure.

The machines, still active, start to reconstruct the figure and form a shiny metallic shell around the limbs of the body. The figure stands up, and its eyes begin to glow.

"ARETMIS has full control of LC-7 and the body has repaired itself," says Lydia. "Arley, are you there?"

"Yes Mom, I'm here and online. I've moved to the location you instructed. The facility is still being monitored and there is security surrounding the area. I'm sure the Board will try to reclaim what they can, even if it's just corrupted data."

"We are fully operational and control is now yours… I want to thank you for saving me, and I want you to know your father was a good man once. I will continue to watch over him, and maybe we can give it another go one day."

"Yeah I'm sure, but for now, it's going to be a lot safer for him to stay where he is. Also, I kind of like hearing your voice all the time Mom. We sure did miss you."

"I know kids. I'm here now thanks to you. ARTEMIS's systems are at maximum output and fully functional. LC-7 has far more power than I expected, especially with your modifications. To think, the Board wanted to fully weaponize this," ARTEMIS says in Lydia's voice.

"Well, they'll get a chance to see it soon enough." The glow of the eyes ceases and the armored figure flashes brightly.

"Let us begin then, shall we?" Alex says as they depart the facility through the front door.

Turning of the Tide

by
Dennis Zambrotta

Planning for this year's annual surfcasting trip to Block Island began in April of 2010. The four of us, known to other surfcasters as "Denny's Crew," were all drawn together by our love of fishing for striped bass. My name is Denny Needlefish from Newport, and my crew are Darter Al from Montauk, The Troll from Brockton, and Tattoo Bob from Billerica. We have personalities as unique as our names. I'm Denny Needlefish because of my propensity to cast Needlefish lures for my quarry. I'm also the informal leader and organizer of this group. I assign everyone a job and give them lists of responsibilities including what food and supplies to bring. When you work for the Department of Defense for forty years, attention to detail and organization come second nature. Now retired, I recently accepted a position working in a subsidiary simulation division for DOD tech giant VirtuTide. I like to write and document the events of each trip. I also tend to be superstitious, especially on fishing trips, a trait of mine the crew mercilessly teases me for.

My friend Darter Al is named for his preference for using Darter lures. Darter is an optometrist and the analytic mind of our group. He picks the places and times to fish, a deduction that he makes based on currents, winds, locations, tides, moon phases, and experience. When ideal conditions are not at hand these decisions are often based on an educated guess, which is Darter Al's way of saying a hunch.

The Troll is named for his membership in an elite group of fishermen called the Ditch Trolls who prowl the waters of the Cape Cod Canal. Troll is a carpenter by trade and the eldest and most experienced of the crew in all aspects of surfcasting. Troll sometimes gets spooked in the dark and prefers to fish with a partner during the dead of night.

The last member of the crew is my good friend Tattoo Bob. Tattoo is a plumber by trade and named for being covered head to toe with tattoos. Tattoo, with a shaved head and all that ink, looks like the meanest son of a bitch in the nastiest biker bar in the world. On the contrary, he is as mild mannered as a kindergarten teacher. But, if ever an intimidator is needed, Tattoo Bob is our man.

Darter scheduled the three-day trip at the very end of October, a time when striped bass would be on their annual migration from New England to their wintering grounds in Chesapeake Bay. This migration path can occur anywhere from several miles off the coast to within a short cast from the shores of Block Island, especially if there is a healthy population of sand eels and herring, the favorite forage of the bass. If our timing was right my crew would have a fruitful trip. If not, it could be an exercise in futility. As Darter often says, "We can't catch what's not here."

Block Island was formed by glaciers and is shaped like a pork chop. It is seven miles long north to south and three miles across at its widest point. It lies thirteen miles off the southern coast of mainland Rhode Island and fourteen miles from Montauk, New York. The island's natural beauty is unmatched, and it is considered one of the last twelve great places in the western hemisphere by The Nature Conservancy. It was first inhabited by the Native Manissean tribe who called it Manisses, meaning "Isle of the Little God." In 1614 it was renamed for the Dutch explorer Adrian Block. Block Island also has some very interesting and somewhat sordid history. At the south end of the island lies the majestic 200-foot high Mohegan Bluffs, so named for an American Indian battle in 1590 when forty members of a Mohegan Tribe raiding party were driven off the bluffs to their deaths by the victorious Manissean Tribe.

The best way to reach Block Island is a ferry ride from Galilee. We all made ferry reservations for our vehicles to arrive at Block on Saturday, October 30. Halloween on the island is a very special event, especially if the night falls on a weekend. Island residents go all out to make the night special for the island's children and visitors. As if the island isn't spooky enough when we are surfcasting at all hours of the night, the islanders dress up as ghouls, monsters, and zombies running tours and hayrides that are downright scary at times. We were really looking forward to this trip!

Though only planning a three-day stay, I'd make sure our vehicles were packed with supplies for almost any contingency, including enough food to feed a small army for a month. With weather, fish, and the sea, you never know exactly how things are going to play out. I like to hope for the best and plan for the worst. For this trip I also left room in my vehicle for some new VirtuTide VR equipment and software to experiment with and hoped to enlist the crew to help me out.

***

As always during our trip the weather is the true wild card. A week before our scheduled departure, a tropical depression formed in the fabled Bermuda Triangle. I watched the Weather Channel constantly. Sure enough, the tropical depression turned into Hurricane Pephredo, and it quickly made a track toward the coast of New England. I wasn't the only one curious about the name Pephredo, a name I'd never heard. I did a little research on Google which turned up the name and its meaning. Pephredo was a name of Greek origin meaning *dread*. Oh shit. Reading it gave me an uneasy feeling. I needed to call the rest of the crew and tell them to keep tabs on this storm as it could very likely impact our fishing and ferry departures. Before I could dial Darter's number my phone rang in my hand with a call from him.

"Did you see the forecast!" he said. "They're predicting a Category 2 hurricane, winds up to 125 from the east/northeast then hard west/northwest. We're going to get blown out! Waves up to twenty feet! The water will be the color of chocolate milk. I think we should cancel our trip."

Part of me felt relief, names being auspicious and all. But we were all looking forward to this trip, and on Halloween weekend. It would be hard to reschedule. Besides, we'd had some fantastic fishing on the back side of big storms on past trips.

"Yes, I've seen the forecast. I think we should hold tight as it may be north of us by Saturday. I'm going to call the Troll and Tattoo and see what they think and get back to you."

I called the Troll and gave him the forecast. As usual, he took the news in stride and just let me make the decisions.

"Denny, whatever you want to do is fine with me, I'll just go with the flow," said Troll.

I called Tattoo and gave him the extended forecast. There was nervousness in his voice. "I don't know Denny, I'm starting to get seasick just listening to the weather reports. I'll get sick and it'll take me days to recover. It will be a game time decision for me. I'll let you know at the end of the week."

Sure enough, Pephredo hit the southern New England coast on Wednesday morning October 27th and lasted until Friday morning the 29th. Ferries to Block Island were canceled from Wednesday through Friday, and then resumed on Saturday just in time for us to get to the island.

***

We met in Galilee to catch the 11:00 a.m. ferry to the island. It was a very rough sail through the remnants of Hurricane Pephredo. Tattoo was loaded with Dramamine, but it had little effect. He spent the entire trip retching in the restroom, only to emerge as we entered Old Harbor on Block. He walked slowly towards where we were sitting, looked down at us and exclaimed, "That was a fucking ferry ride from hell."

After the ferry docked, we drove to the Neptune House apartment which would serve as home for the next three days. The local businesses and homes were all decked out with jack-o'-lanterns, skeletons, ghosts, and ghouls. It was always an amazing sight.

After unpacking we took a ride around the island to survey the storm damage and scout for any signs of fish. The hurricane had smacked the island with quite a wallop—trees and downed limbs everywhere, and a few sailboats washed ashore in the salt pond. I had expected the water to look like chocolate milk, but it was becoming clearer by the minute thanks to the brisk westerly wind coming off the backside of the storm. We spent the rest of the day gearing up for a long night of surfcasting. Our anticipation was high and the surf was calming by the hour.

Just before dinner my phone rang. It was John, my department head at VirtuTide.

"Hi Denny, I got your email about running the new VR scenario on Block Island. Talked it over with the division and we approved letting you run it for your friends, if they agree."

Not wanting the crew to hear my reply I moved outside the front door before responding.

"That's great news. I'm sure they'll agree. I might even run some of the new scenarios if I feel conditions are right."

"Fine, just be careful. Hope you guys have a great time and catch the big one!"

***

For our first night of fishing, we agreed to split up in pairs so we could scout and cover more island locations. Tattoo and Troll would head to Mansion Beach. Darter and I would start at Black Rock on the south side of the island.

Me and Darter half-hiked and half-slid down the 200-foot bluff towards one of our favorite haunts along this stretch of Block Island shore. Once at the base of the cliff we headed west toward the periodic flash of Montauk Light on the distant horizon. Our destination was False Point, a name we gave to a nondescript clump of rocks that formed a small boulder field. Very few other island regulars fished False Point, but we knew from many years of experience that there were times when it was the only place with feeding bass, especially after a storm.

It was close to midnight and the half-moon cast a glowing light along the rocky shore. Our first three hours of casting were uneventful, a far cry from the previous year's trip to the island when we both had fish on our first cast. The wind had calmed, and the surf had a gentle swell, just enough to hear the clatter of cobblestone as each wave receded. The incoming tide was just starting to flood and would begin to push water onto False Point with a left to right sweep.

Clad in wetsuits, we waded to our favorite flat rocks and began casting Needlefish plugs into the submerged boulder field. Twenty more minutes of casting produced no strikes. I glanced over my left shoulder towards Darter. Darter struck the familiar stance of a surfcaster fighting a good fish—knees bent, back arched, and fishing rod bowed double. The slight tug of a strike on my lure pulled my attention back to my stretch of water as thirty pounds of striped bass exploded on the water's surface not ten feet from my perch. A short battle with a tight drag and I had this fish at my feet, slid her onto my perch, removed the treble hooks, and sent her back into the water for a successful catch and release.

Darter yelled, "How big?"

"Around thirty."

"Mine was about the same."

We both hooked up again on our next cast and released another pair of thirty-pound class fish. Eight-inch sand eels skimmed across the surface just beyond my perch. A little further out, swirls of giant bass pursued them. We continued to catch and release bass for the next hour until the flooding tide and surf forced us back. The final tally was eleven bass for Darter and eight for me. Feeling very content, we decided to end the night early and get some well-deserved sleep.

Thoroughly exhausted, Darter and I trudged along the mile walk back to the truck, all the while savoring the great action we had experienced. About fifty yards from the bluff trail, I spotted a familiar shape lying in the tangled seaweed and driftwood of the wrack line. Years of walking the beach have honed my vision so I can spot a lost lure washed ashore on even the darkest of nights. The lime green color reflected the light of the moon.

"Darter, look, a Super Strike Needlefish."

"Hey, there's another one," Darter said, pointing just ahead.

"Mine looks brand new; hooks have no rust."

Darter trotted over to his prize.

"Same with mine. I bet they fell out of someone's surf bag. Poor guy just lost forty bucks."

I stooped to pick up my newfound needle when I heard Darter screech in pain. He looked at me for help, his expression full of terror as he ran, twisting and turning toward the bluff. The lure in my hand jerked and the treble hooks ripped into my palm. Searing pain raced up my arm. What the hell is happening? The warmth of my own blood enveloped my cold hand. I struggled to tear free of the hooks embedded in my palm and fingers, but I could not gain release from the barbed hook points. I gathered my senses and my mangled hand jerked toward the surf. The lure in my hand was attached to a taut line that led into the water. Something was reeling me in.

I clutched the lure tight and ran towards the bluff. I fought for each step but only gained a few dozen yards before my muscles tired. I screamed as the line snapped tight and pulled back towards the water's edge. The harder I struggled to rid myself of the hooks, the deeper they bit into my hand. My blood dotted the sand in a dark trail as I struggled and strained for purchase. Closer and closer to the water I slid. The soft gravel at the surf's edge shifted under my weight, and I fell and slid into the wash. I glimpsed Darter running to my aid, the needlefish lure still stuck in his left thumb, then the line pulled me under. Darter plunged into the surf after me and grappled with my coat and arms until he managed to cut the line on my lure with a pair of pliers he kept tethered on his lure bag. We both fell to the beach exhausted and bloodied from the battle.

"What is happening? Are you okay?" I yelled.

Darter pointed seaward toward something about thirty feet out. There, right next to one of our favorite rock perches, were two huge striped bass, each holding a surf rod and frantically tying on another lure, one guaranteed to fool even the wariest of surfcasters.

"They're fishing for us! Let's get the fuck out of here!" yelled Darter.

We ran back towards the bluff as two more needlefish landed off to our sides. We dared not touch them. The wail of my truck's horn grew louder and louder as I climbed the trail. My truck parked where I left it, headlights on and cabin dark. I grabbed the door handle, but it wouldn't open. Panic rushed over me and I yanked and pounded on the handle. Finally, the door gave way, and I woke up to the scream of my phone alarm in my hand.

I shook the cobwebs out of my head. The dream was too real. It's not unusual for me to have fish dreams, but they are seldom as realistic as this. It was so real I was shaking. I looked at my hands for injuries, but my skin was unblemished. I sat in bed for a while pondering the dream and its meaning. All I could think was to call it a "revenge fantasy" dream. Do fish dream?

I went to wake up the crew. It was six AM, and time to head out for the turn of the tide to catch a few bass. And maybe, if we're lucky, find a lure or two, though maybe I'd let others pick them up this time.

***

I told the crew about my dream while we were having breakfast. Of course, everyone was amused and as usual started to poke fun at me.

"Well at least *something* was caught last night. Troll and I never even saw a bass," Tattoo joked.

"Denny, thanks for reminding me of why I don't fish with you and Darter. Never a dull night with you two. Even in your dreams there is way too much drama for me," said Troll.

Darter smiled over his coffee. "Well, that's certainly a turn of the tide. The striped bass finally got revenge on you. The animal rights groups will love it."

I huffed and brought my plate to the sink. "I guess you're right; and thank you all very much for the ball-busting."

But something about this nightmare really bothered me. I already had a bad feeling about this trip with the foreboding hurricane, and this nightmare just added to my anxiety.

After breakfast we spent Sunday morning fishing at a few more locations. We went to one of my favorite areas near Vail Beach, a spot called Snake Hole. It was a beautiful area on the south end of the island that lies below the infamous 200-foot-high Mohegan Bluffs.

We parked in the dirt lot above Snake Hole. There are two trails down the bluff.

"Ok, make sure to take the trail down on your right, never use the left trail going down." I instructed.

"Wait, what? Why?" asked Tattoo.

"Listen, you know the old saying that when you come to two trails you always take the "right" one?" I've always done this on Block. I took the left trail down once and sprained my ankle. Ever since I've taken the right trail. When we come back up, we will take the trail on our right which will be this left trail, so we'll get to use both. But we must use them in the right sequence."

"Jesus Denny, you're nuts." laughed Darter.

Troll rolled his eyes and in a hushed voice replied to the others, "Par for the course when fishing with Denny."

While walking the beach we came across the remains of the hulk of an old wooden shipwreck, part of it severely charred and half buried in the sand. We were intrigued by the discovery and started to look for anything we could find to identify the wreck and maybe provide a keepsake. Darter found a square headed nail that had us speculating about the age of the ship. Troll found a baseball-sized piece of coal. Tattoo dug around the sand until he found an old coin with an inscription that was difficult to decipher.

Darter squinted at the coin trying to make out the inscription, "Wow, it looks like a skull and crossbones."

"Really?" replied Tattoo.

Darter snorted a laugh. "Geez Tattoo, you're so damn gullible. It's not pirate booty. I can only make out three letters EIN, the others are indecipherable."

My unease went into high gear. The wreck looked old, all waterlogged wood and what little metal was left was very corroded. "This wreck could have been uncovered from the erosion caused by Hurricane Dread. You know a coal barge sunk after a collision with a US submarine in 1945 near here. I think it's better to leave this undisturbed until the authorities can look at it. And I might add, taking historic artifacts is against the law and could bring us bad luck."

Tattoo snidely remarked, "Well maybe we should all just get the hell of this island before something bad happens."

The rest of the crew ignored my advice and took the items back to the apartment, much to my chagrin.

That afternoon while we watched the New England Patriots defeat the Minnesota Vikings, I went on my laptop to research the island's history of shipwrecks. I read about the Annapolis coal barge incident, as well as steamships which sank just offshore over the years that could possibly explain the items found by the crew. I read about an event in 1690 when French pirates attacked the island and were repelled by islanders. And in 1738 the British ship *Palatine*, carrying 240 immigrants and a crew of fourteen from the Palatine region of southwest Germany, was shipwrecked after being driven ashore by a snowstorm.

One version of this story described the crew rowing a lifeboat ashore and leaving their passengers aboard the *Palatine* to drown. Block Island residents then persuaded the crew to bring all 150 of the passengers who had survived the transatlantic voyage ashore. The residents nursed them to health in their own homes and later retrieved their possessions. The islanders also buried about twenty passengers who died in the wreck, and in 1947 the Block Island Historical Society put a marker at the site of the *Palatine* graves.

Another more sordid version of this story claimed that islanders had lured the *Palatine* to sail onto the shallow shoals with a false navigation light. Then they murdered the starving, freezing passengers and crew and looted the cargo. They set the *Palatine* on fire and pushed it back out to sea to hide their crime. The story became the legend of the *Palatine* ghost ship. Some island residents say that the *Palatine* ghost ship still appears in flames at night off the Block Island coast.

I related all this information to the crew. But the guys were into the game and barely acknowledged me. I decided to share the information I uncovered with my company as it could be useful for scenarios we were working on in immersive virtual reality. Still, a part of me was itching to throw that coal back into the surf when Troll wasn't looking.

After the Pats game we enjoyed a hearty beef stew made for us by Tattoo's wife Julie. Bellies full, we geared up for another night of surfcasting. The plan was for Troll and Tattoo to cover the areas near the morning's shipwreck discovery: Snake Hole, Barlow's Point, and Black Rock. Darter and I would cast the area about a half mile west at Lewis Point. It was 4:30 p.m.. Just outside the apartment the island residents were celebrating Halloween. "Monster Mash" was playing on an outside speaker just next door.

Kids and adults all dressed up in costume were already going door to door trick-or-treating. Just before entering our vehicles a commotion ran through the crowd. Trick-or-treaters turned in clusters and pointed up at the sky. The blaze of a meteor streaked across the dark sky from north to south. What set it apart from other meteors I had witnessed in the past was that it lasted for a full fifteen seconds before breaking apart in a fiery display. Everyone stood in awe as we watched it fizzle out.

I couldn't take my eyes off the sky. What the hell was that? Meteor, space station, satellite? The island children were all excited and yelling, "UFO!"

Was it just another mysterious wonder on this island that always seemed full of them? Or was it something else that entered the atmosphere? My logical self was thinking meteor, but my superstitious side sensed something different. I felt uneasy, my mind raced, and it was all starting to add up: Hurricane Dread, my nightmare, and now this. What else could possibly happen? I knew the crew could see it on my face. Then I thought that this could be the perfect time to set my planned software experiment into motion, albeit with a twist.

"You alright Denny? You look like you've seen a ghost," asked Tattoo.

"Thanks guys, I'm alright, just feeling the effects of not getting much sleep last night.

I think I'm going to skip casting with you tonight, at least until I get my second wind. Maybe I'll join you later. I'm sorry Darter, but you'll have to fish with Troll and Tattoo tonight. But before I forget I have something new from my company for all of you to try tonight. Believe me, you'll love it. It's experimental and will really help us get some real time data for a VR fishing game. And who knows, some of you might even catch the record-breaking striped bass of your dreams. I'll just need to clip it to your head lamps before you head out and start fishing."

"Sure, anything you can do to help because lord knows I just can't seem to catch big bass. Hope you feel better and get some rest," replied Tattoo.

"We'll make sure to tell any ghosts we meet that you said hello," joked Darter.

"Oh, I'm sure you will." I replied as I clipped a VARP10 unit to each of their headlamps.

***

The trio of Darter, Troll, and Tattoo then headed out for a night of fishing on this porkchop-shaped island. They turned down Snake Hole Road and parked in a small clearing next to the trail down the bluffs. One by one they looked up into the night sky at the barely discernible contrail which ended at the water's surface a few hundred yards out from shore. The air temperature at the south side hollow had dropped into the mid-twenties and a fine coating of frost on the scrub brush sparkled eerily in the light of their head lamps.

Troll pointed at the trail in the sky. "Darter, look at that."

"Geez Troll, it's only a vapor trail. We see them all the time when we're fishing at night," Darter said.

"Yea, but this one enters the water just offshore."

"Troll you're starting to act paranoid like Denny. It's the night sky playing tricks on your eyes. Come on, let's go catch some bass." Tattoo marched ahead.

A few hours of casting at the cobble's edge saw the striped bass striking black Super Strike Needlefish and Redfin lures retrieved at the slowest of speeds. Little did they know, with the help of the VARP units the twenty to twenty-five-pound bass the crew were catching were manipulated to appear to be fifty to fifty-five pounds. The crew were having the bite of their lives. Every hookup produced a bass larger than before.

"This is unbelievable… and fun!" exclaimed Troll as a hookup with a huge bass dragged him down the beach past Darter and Tattoo, who were attached to their own bass going in different directions.

"This bite is going to provide great data for Denny," said Darter.

"Denny's company will have a winning product. I'm calling him after I land this bass to tell him how good the bite is. This is too good to miss! He needs to get out here," replied Tattoo.

***

Back at the Neptune House I monitored what was happening in real time via my laptop. My screen was partitioned into three separate displays to show what Troll, Darter, and Tattoo were seeing and experiencing. I controlled each of their VARP10 units with the help of the hologram software and my input. Then my phone rang.

"Denny, this is Tattoo. If you're feeling any better you need to get out here now. The bite we're having is fucking unbelievable!"

"Oh man, thanks for the report. I am feeling a little better. How big are the bass?"

"Every fish has been over forty. Some over fifty! I've never witnessed anything like this," Tattoo replied.

"OK, I'll gear up ASAP. Should be down there to join you guys in about thirty minutes."

I hung up and immediately got back on my laptop to embed the zombie scenario hologram software into the VARP units. Finally, I had the chance to play the joker and get back at the guys for teasing me all the time.

***

After his call with Denny, Tattoo ran towards Darter to get back in on the action.

"Darter, I just called Denny. He's feeling better and will be here shortly."

"Awesome. This bite is epic. I'd hate to see him miss it."

Two a.m. came swiftly with an unexplained glow about 200 yards out from Black Rock Point. Darter reeled in his line while peering at the glow. "Could it be one of those crazy fishermen that fishes while they're swimming? I think they're called skishers?"

"No way with the strong currents out there," said Tattoo.

They watched as the glow went on and off and from white to red. It started out looking like a navigation light but became almost flame-like as it grew closer to the beach. Then it vanished. A short while later a glint of moonlight betrayed unusual movement at the surf's edge. Darter pointed his head light to illuminate a half dozen people walking out of the water. At first glance their garments seemed to hang off them in strange strips and tatters, and they didn't look like other fishermen as Darter expected.

167

Despite their appearance Darter yelled at them, "Have any luck?"

They didn't respond. Their shadows jerked and flickered eerily across the sand in the low light with their awkward shambling gaits. Darter's gut clenched with fear.

"Hey Darter, where's Troll?" asked Tattoo.

"He told me he wanted to go cast further down the shoreline, near the wreck we found today."

The strangers drew closer, and their grunting, unintelligible sounds carried over the surf. Tattoo and Darter backed away as the strangers stretched their hands out to reach for them across the shrinking distance.

"Who… what are they? What did they say? Maybe this is a Halloween prank? A weird flash mob?" asked Darter.

"I don't know. I couldn't make out anything but grunts. I've known islanders that have done some weird shit, but this water is really cold for a prank. Let's get out of here."

Tattoo hightailed it down the beach toward Troll with Darter at his heels.

***

Troll was casting near the wreck and snagged his line on what he thought was the bottom. He jerked his rod back and forth trying to free the lure and faintly felt the snag pull back.

"Could this be a fish?" he muttered to himself. When the snag kept moving but didn't swim away he figured it was just some rockweed and pulled really hard until the lure freed itself. A mass of ripped cloth and tangled seaweed clung to the hooks. "What the hell is this?" he thought. As he struggled to remove the cloth he squeezed a firm lump through the tangle. He picked off a few more scraps of cloth and vegetation and uncovered a bloated, rotting finger. He flung the lump down with a yelp. A violent splashing interrupted the rhythmic lap of the surf on the shore. He spun and turned on his head light. The beam illuminated a commercial fisherman tangled in rope struggling to get out of the water. Troll sprang into action and jumped off his perch. "Hey man, you hurt? Hold up, I've got you."

Troll waded into the surf and offered the stranger a helpful hand. An unintelligible grunt stopped him mid stride. Troll scrambled back, legs shaking with fear.

"Troll?" Tattoo yelled.

Troll lunged out of the surf as the creature flailed and thrashed behind him in the water. "Zombie!" he cried.

"Zombie?"

"It just tried to grab me!" Troll raced by Tattoo and Darter, boots kicking up sand and gravel in his wake. In the distance beyond Troll's fishing spot more hollow-eyed figures crawled from the surf.

"They're not carrying fishing rods," said Tattoo.

Darter followed his gaze. "Let's get the hell out of here."

They ran along the base of the bluffs towards the trail to the parking area, the lumbering strangers in pursuit. As they rounded a huge boulder another zombie lurched from the ground. Troll tripped over a rock in panic. Darter and Tattoo helped Troll back just as the zombie reached for them. Two more gruesome decomposed beings emerged from the water.

Finally at the parking area they briefly looked down from the bluff, the strangers slowly clawing and crawling up the trail while even more dark shapes emerged from the surf.

Darter barked out orders as they scrambled to get into the truck. "Lock the doors and stay away from the windows! Call Denny and tell him what happened and that we're on our way back. Then call 911!"

As Tattoo jumped into the truck his head hit the roof, knocking off his head light.

"Hurry up! They're almost here!" screamed Troll.

Tattoo looked outside and didn't see any more zombies. Darter and Troll continued to look toward the trailhead with terrified stares. Something didn't add up. Tattoo put his headlamp back on and the zombies were back. Took it off and they were gone. He reached over and pulled off Darter's headlamp, then grabbed Trolls. Once the headlamps were off everything became calm. They looked at each other in nervous disbelief.

"Guys, we were pranked. Put your headlamps back on for a second."

Troll put his headlamp back on, screamed, and then immediately took it off. Darter did the same and began to giggle.

"Denny and his company are behind this. He got us good," said Darter.

"Fishing software my ass," replied Troll. "Let's get back and give him hell."

***

Back at the cottage I monitored the final moments of the zombie scenario with glee. If it wasn't for Tattoo accidentally knocking off his headlamp this scenario would have continued on their ride back. I waited to greet them upon their return.

They pulled into the driveway of the apartment and noticed that my vehicle was still parked outside. I sat looking out the apartment window and turned my attention to the front door.

The guys walked in and I couldn't help but start laughing. They were half pissed and half smiling. It was apparent the VirtuTide scenario programmed into the headlamp attachment worked well—maybe too well.

Troll was first to break the silence. "Zombies, Denny? I mean really? You couldn't just stick with fish?"

"Well Troll, at least we caught the biggest bass of our lives tonight," Darter laughed.

"Calm down guys. Let me explain what you experienced. Remember the VirtuTide attachment I added to your headlamps? Well, it's called VARP10 which stands for Virtual Alternate Reality Pod. We've been working on it for a while, and you are the first to experience the Surfcaster/Zombie encounter scenario, which was my idea."

"What are you talking about?" interrupted Tattoo.

"Just about everything you witnessed tonight while fishing was all a virtual scenario programmed into the VARP. Our idea was to collect data about the surfcasting experience, visual and emotional. Being placed near your temple it's able to monitor your vital signs and present holograms in your sightlines. It also has the capability to alter what you're viewing. For instance, all those big bass you caught tonight were much smaller than they appeared to you as you landed them. The VARP seemed to work perfectly as far as I could monitor."

"Monitor?" asked Tattoo.

"Yes, I used my laptop to monitor your real time experiences, reactions, blood pressure, and heart rate to make sure nothing bad happened. I was also able to control what you were "seeing" at times.

"Geez Denny! It was way too realistic! You could have at least warned us!" said Troll.

"I know, but we already beta tested it with a group of volunteer surfcasters fishing on Nantucket. Because they were volunteers, we had to tell them what we were doing and what they would experience. Because they knew what would happen it became just another boring Virtual Reality experience. My idea was to test it on you because we've all been longtime friends and I know what you can handle. I convinced the company we could gather data that was not skewed by knowing participants. If I told you what to expect, your experience and reactions would have been very different. For us at VirtuTide, the best data always comes from surprise, and for the user the best experience comes from surprise as well."

After a long silence Darter asked, "Wow, well done. But are you sure you didn't have an ulterior motive?"

"Well, you guys are always teasing me. There isn't a year that goes by that you don't rib me to death. I originally planned to just goof on you guys by making you think you were catching world-class sized bass, but after what happened at the wreck site yesterday, I just knew I had to add the zombie scenario. And boy I am glad I did. It was hilarious watching all of you. I got the idea for it from *The Walking Dead* and pitched it as a "Turning of the Tide" scenario that takes place on a quiet off-season island, with surfcasting as a dark, desolate shoreline nighttime activity. I thought Block Island would be a perfect setting. I can't wait to hear feedback from the company execs. I really want to thank you for participating and being great friends. What did you think of it?"

"I'm still a little pissed, but it was kind of funny in retrospect," responded Troll.

"It may go down as the ultimate ball bust of all time. And you can be sure we won't be letting you anywhere near our headlamps ever again," added Tattoo.

"Alright guys, get some sleep and rest up. We have one more day and night to catch some bass. Thanks again for your understanding."

***

Just after breakfast I received a call from John, my department head.

"Denny, this is John. Our team just went over the scenario from last night. We have a concern. I'm not sure if you saw this when you were watching your laptop out there but a tech noticed your friend Troll snag up on something then take what appeared to be cloth and weeds off his hooks. Immediately afterwards there was grunting coming from the zombie holograms."

"Yeah, I remember that part of the recording."

"Problem is, tech didn't add sound to the program yet. We are still analyzing the data but you need to immediately cease additional experiments."

My stomach tightened. "Yes sir, will do." I hung up. I looked at the guys.

"Denny, you look sick again. Is everything OK at home?" asked Darter.

173

"Troll, did you get snagged up last night?"

"Yeah, I did Denny. It was weird. There was cloth on my hooks, and it looked like an old Colonial shirt with a severed finger in it. You've got a sick imagination, man."

I didn't know what to say. That I'd constructed this whole zombie scenario but I hadn't made that?

"Holy shit guys, look." Darter turned up the volume on the news.

Police cruisers and emergency vehicles studded the shoreline near Snake Hole. The sky was the twisting gray of a building storm.

"Oh shit."

Back from Iraq

by
Vincent A Scirocco Jr

The Broken Soldier

The sirens have sounded.
The whistles have blown.
This sadness takes over
that he's never known.
The bullets set rhythm.
The bombs set the tone.
As his friends rush to battle,
he sits there alone.

He can't watch them leave.
He can't bear the sight
or the thought that he may
not see them tonight.

He constantly thinks,
"Did I do all I could?"
As they mounted the trucks
by his door he just stood,
knowing in this condition
he'd do them no good.

With questions unanswered,
it's to God that he prays:
"Please give me the reason

I sit here today."

The thought that he's stuck there,
it fills him with rage.
Like a lion with no pride
that is stuck in a cage.
Or an actor, not needed,
always standing backstage.
Words are his outlet
as he fills this page.

Some say he'll get better
in no time at all,
that he'll play in the game
and he'll carry the ball.
These are just words
in sentences they're small.
They help give him hope
and help him to stand tall.

Others may doubt
he will ever return.
He prays for them
that they never learn
the feelings inside him,
the way that they burn.

He sits there and ponders
what his future brings.
"Will I lose all hope?
Will they cut all my strings?

Or will we fly together
as I spread my wings?"

Only time will tell
as they measure and test.
Will his body perform
and fit in with the rest?
Will he earn all the medals
that belong on his chest?
Or will he be airborne
on a plane headed west?

No matter the outcome
he can say that he's tried.
That he did all he could
to stay on for the ride.
If he must return home
he will do so with pride.
But he'll do so while feeling
his hands have been tied.

No welcome was waiting.
No one knew his name.
With his hope quickly fading,
his head bowed in shame.
It's hard to keep hating
when there's no one to blame.

With testing complete
he'll be waiting no more.
They'll treat his injuries

once he's processed to shore.
His departure's discreet
as he walks out the door.
Just his wife there to greet him
as the tears start to pour.

His history shows
that he did his best.
He himself knows
he gave nothing less.
He'll get rid of his patch
when it's ripped off his chest.
They fill him with meds.
They downplay his pain.
Evil thoughts in his head
become hard to restrain.

Am I better off dead?
He thinks again and again
while he's lying in bed
staring hard at his vein.
Am I guilty? He asks.
Is there someone to blame?
While friends offer flasks
thus confirming his shame.
Now so many wear masks
things will never be the same.

He did what was requested.
He did so with pride.
When his body was tested,

BACK FROM IRAQ

God knows how he tried.

Some say he got bested
and perhaps wish he died.
He could never have guessed
who'd remain by his side.

They offer nearly zero
for all eighteen years.
A gift for a hero
that can't walk up stairs.

All the things he was told,
everything he worked for
he can no longer hold.
They lie scattered on the floor.

Twenty years have come and passed.
My God, how time can fly!
The sands inside the glass
track time that's passed by.
Amazing how some friendships crack
without knowing why.
While there are those who have his back
until the day he dies.

A sense of debt he holds
regardless what he can provide.
As each page of life unfolds
it's quickly brushed off to the side.
Now he's growing old,

only God knows how he's tried
to pay back what is owed,
a constant debt that won't subside.

Over time he has learned
several ways to compensate.
He has worked and he has earned
everything that's on his plate.
He has watched candles burn,
felt the heat from the flames of fate.
The Broken Soldier has returned.
Let us pray he's not too late.

He has realized his debts were paid
a long, long time ago.
As no debt was really made,
he is the only one he owed.

In every rabbit hole he's chased
and all he's come to know,
he has found a sense of grace
and hopes to never let it go.

By shiny days blessed by the sun
or days it might rain,
there's hope and joy for everyone
a chance to live again.
Sometimes the struggle isn't fun.
At times we all feel pain.
Yet it's through struggle every victory's won;
without it there's no gain.

BACK FROM IRAQ

He has heard so many times
It is the dark that shows the light:
so many words, so many rhymes, so many lines of sight.
Though many years have passed him by,
there's still some time to write.
The Broken Soldier, he was I, and I will be alright.

United We Will Stand

Since before we were a nation
there have always been the few
that combat deprivation
and ensure our freedom's true.
From the great emancipation
and all the wars that we've been through
they get our admiration.
It is the least that we can do.

Whether serving in the states
or in some very distant land,
their sacrifice is great.
I'm sure you understand.
One should never hesitate
to offer them the kindest hand.
It is they who guard the gate
and protect our promised land.

No, freedom is not free;
we all shoulder the cost.
Over land, by sky and sea
many valiant lives were lost.
Lost eternally
through years and through the wars.
Lost for you and me
and lost for freedom's cause.

To those standing in harm's way
and those still under command,

BACK FROM IRAQ

those who simply signed away
the very life that they had planned,
those that couldn't stay
and those not asked to stand,
all the families as they pray
and all supporters across the land,
it's with great passion that I say
in the utmost way I can
Thank you all this Veterans Day
and as united we will stand.

VINCENT SCIROCCO

Lucidity

A sunlit day begins
in a small New England town.
A doctor shuffles in
and asks us all to gather 'round.
He spends some time explaining the compound.
"I'm sure you will be fine once you take a look around.

"You have all volunteered
to help us find a cure."
Every word the doctor shared
made me feel less secure.

We were seven vets selected
from the VA's MVP.
Veterans' blood that they collected
provided DNA for free.
I would never have expected
one selected would be me.

"Relax," we all are told.
"I'll explain why you are here.
Your minds have all been sold;
reprogrammed with great care.
You are just a few days old.
Your memories, you all share."

It seemed that we had died,
each of us in our own way.
We faced the great divide,

yet we're standing here today.
Our deaths we were denied
and with life we've been repaid.
Now we all must hide
since to rest we were once laid.

I might have had a wife.
I cannot say for sure.
The moments of my life
are an inconsistent blur.
I'm convinced I used a knife
to end the pain that I endured.
My sickness was my life
and so my death became the cure.

"You're free to roam the grounds
that were designed using your psych.
It is not a large compound,
and you may partake in what you like.
You can simply walk around
or you can take a longer hike.
Your cabins can be found
on the south side of the pike.

"I know this may sound
a little hard to believe.
Your DNA was wound,
as such, your life could be retrieved.
You must stay on these grounds.
You must not ever try to leave.
It's really quite profound

that from your death you have been freed."

We soon were let go
to find our cabins near the road.
Somehow we would know
which one was ours' though never told.
At first, we took it slow
accepted things as they'd unfold.
We were going with the flow.
Still in our minds they had a hold.

Each cabin was built for one.
It had everything you'd need.
Ammo with a gun,
and a barrel full of mead.
Fishing poles were hung
near a satchel full of weed.
I anticipated fun
more than I could have believed.

The dwellings formed a ring
about one mile wide.
In the center we could bring
anything we'd decide.
The nightly gathering
was where we could confide,
where we'd share most anything,
except for how we'd died.

I didn't see the harm.
I shared with them my name.

BACK FROM IRAQ

I said "Hi, my name is Tom"
and learned theirs beside the flame.
The biggest guy was Rom.
His demeanor seemed quite tame.
While Oscar had some charm,
he seemed to hide a sense of shame.

Uriah was soft spoken,
while Brien seldom spoke.
Though their lives were broken,
they could both tell a joke.
Larry had the strangest token
he wore much like a yoke.
Leather necklace, tightly woven;
any tighter, he might choke.

Ed was kind of thin,
sort of frail, and quite tall.
Although he wore a grin
it seemed he'd built a wall.
He hadn't any kin,
at least none he could recall.
He heard voices from within
and tried to listen to them all.

It was a beautiful retreat.
The perfect place to get some rest.
We had plenty there to eat.
Uriah claimed he cooked the best.
We could hunt to gather meat
or fish the pond out to our west.

VINCENT SCIROCCO

Our tribal circle was complete
until the first became possessed.

From towards the fire that first night
there arose such a scream.
Running towards the firelight
it felt more like a dream.
Rom and Brien were in a fight,
maybe just to blow off steam.
Brien's knife cut just right,
and Rom's blood flowed like a stream.

With Rom on the ground,
We thought for sure he was dead.
Ed and I both laid him down
and put sheets over his head.
Brien's hands we quickly bound,
his eyes turned to fiery red.
Then he spoke without a sound,
and this is what he said:

"Foolish mortals listen well,
your time is overspent.
Your souls you could not sell:
they were already spent.
Your empty vessels I can smell,
you all reek of malevolence.
Your elders spoke of living hell.
You will soon know what they meant."

With this his eyes changed back to blue.

BACK FROM IRAQ

He was shocked by what he saw.
He didn't have a clue
why so much blood was on the floor.
We discussed what we should do,
and since I drew the shortest straw,
I'd report what we went through
to the doctor or the law.

We had no phone with which
I could have simply made a call.
The dirt road was slightly pitched.
At times, my pace was a crawl.
I tried to pick up pace
which felt like running up a wall.
When I finally reached the place,
it was like nothing I recalled.

The sun began to rise.
Through the gates it spread its rays.
I was somewhat paralyzed.
For several minutes I just gazed.
Much to my surprise,
although we'd only been here days,
the place was in demise,
left for years to decay.

Like a nightmare in the making
the place had really gone to hell.
It seemed that we had been forsaken.
There was no one there to tell.
When I entered, I was shaking

as each room looked like a cell.
I found a notebook worth taking
and grabbed it just as well.

The book contained some tests
that showed how we were brought back.
Why we were chosen from the rest,
what we had the others lacked.
To understand, I did my best.
It's like my mind had been hacked.
Was that how Brien became possessed?
Is that why Rom had been attacked?

A part of me has learned
you're better off to share the ball.
I would rather wait my turn
than put my back against the wall.
Just as I had turned
to make my way back down the hall,
the others grew concerned
and wondered if I made a call.

"Tommy is not back," said Larry.
"He should've never gone alone.
Oscar, Ed, and I
will check the clinic for a phone.
Uriah stay with Brien
until the risks are better known.
Ensure that he stays tied,"
Larry spoke in a deep tone.

"They take control," says Larry
trying harder to describe.
"That shit with Rom was scary.
It could happen to our tribe.
You all have guns, so carry
if you wish to stay alive.
When troubled souls are wary,
demon spirits sense their vibe.

"With us it's not the same.
There is no soul for them to take.
No spirit left to blame
and no hearts are left to break.
When they feel that sense of shame,
realizing their mistake,
they will call out Satan's name
cause in this world they'll have no stake."

I heard them all approaching
so I met them at the gate.
I spoke like I was coaching
as I made the others wait.
"The clinic is not just closed
it's as if we're a decade late."

With nothing making sense
the others chose to go inside.
As they each crawled through the fence,
I wondered how they might have died.
Was it of a consequence
they could've changed, had they survived?

Or were their problems so intense
they, just as I, chose suicide?

There was nothing left intact
yet several years we did not spend.
Although they brought us back
we all could die again.
We made a solemn pact
to stick together till the end.

Oscar raised his gun
and he aimed it right at me.
With nowhere I could run
I slowly got down on one knee,
knowing for certain I was done
and yet relieved I would be free.

Oscar's eyes were burning red.
His facial features became blurred.
I slowly bowed my head,
then a single shot was heard.
He'd shot himself instead
then spoke without a word.
"All the lies that you were fed;
death has never been a cure.

"You stupid little mortals,
you will never understand.
We use you all like portals
to destroy your fellow man.
We infiltrate your thoughts

to make you follow our command.
Nothing you have brought
can ever keep us from our plan."

I thought, why was I spared?
Why'd he shoot himself instead?
Then straight at me he stared,
"It's your life you once did dread?
Now your misery you'll share!"
Oscar raved and then fell dead.

I hid the notes inside my coat
to keep the pages whole.
I hoped that maybe someone wrote
some way to save my soul.
Although there were no files
in the clinic with a name,
the book contained some trials,
most of which they couldn't tame.
Amongst the thousands of denials
only seven were the same.

The more I read the worse it got.
How was it we were born?
My memories left out a lot.
My emotions left me torn.
It seemed more like the movie plots
where actors don't belong.
I wondered, were we just robots
whose programming went wrong?

Just as it began to seem
that everything might be alright,
Larry jumped up as he screamed
"There is no way to win this fight.
Of this symbol I have dreamed.
It means the vanquishing of light.
In your book it shows a beam."
His speech was affected by his fright.

"I can't explain how I know,
I just know we won't survive.
These notebooks kind of show
how the dead can be alive.
The DNA they grow
then they change it by design.
Like plants that farmers sow
our spirits, taken as they shine."

"Wait a sec," Ed asked,
"we can hear without a sound?
It's like sunlight that is cast;
I kind of feel it all around.
My mind is very vast,
much more open, much less bound."
He continued speaking fast,
"Is it the mead we're guzzling down?"

"How'd it make you feel?"
I asked Brien by the side.
"Did anything seem real?
Know in me you can confide."

"Much like someone took the wheel
and then took me out for a ride,"
Brien stated with great zeal.
How he felt, he did not hide.

In the morning we would rise
to yet another dreadful find.
Brien, much to our surprise,
found himself a piece of twine.
In an oak tree he made ties
around his neck, you know the kind.
I wondered if Brien's demise
was a sense of guilt or loss of mind.

"We must figure out a plan,
I said, "to stop what takes control.
If we find the signal's band,
then we can ground it to a pole.
I finally understand:
the frequency is of our soul.
That's why the spirits are so mad
and it is what the doctor stole."

Finally things made sense
and there was pride in what we did.
We cut down some old fence
that we would shape into a grid.
Then things got quite intense.
Ed asked Uriah, "What's wrong kid?"
Uriah's innocence
into the darkness quickly slid.

VINCENT SCIROCCO

Uriah grabbed a stone
with a supernatural kind of speed.
Towards Edward it was thrown.
It struck his head and made him bleed.
"You fool, you should have known
that in the end you can't succeed.
You aren't human, you're a clone.
You were created from a seed."

He continued stoning Ed
until we finally made him stop.
Blood was gushing from his head
and to the ground he quickly dropped.
With his eyes still shining red,
at himself Uriah chopped.
Within moments both lay dead
with Uriah on the top.

"We have to finish this,"
I told Larry, "we must try."
If we catch the evilness
in this antenna we'll get by.
We cannot afford to miss,
or both of us will surely die.
I think we're good with this
if their signal's not too high.

We dug a plot for Ed
and Uriah side by side.
Then made sure we got fed

with the food we were supplied.
I asked Larry what was said
when I was not by the fireside.
He just smiled and instead
showed me his token with great pride.

The token Larry carried
was the first one that I saw.
It didn't mean that he was married.
It wasn't love that it was for.
I could not stop from further query
and so I pushed a little more.
I knew that Larry could still hear me.
I was growing kind of sore.

"What is with that token
that you're wearing all the time?"
Larry's voice was clearly spoken,
"I only know that it is mine."
It had a circle with a spoke
that crosses through a wavy line.
"I was wearing it when I woke,
but I don't recognize the sign."

"I feel it is a key," he said,
"to what I am not sure.
I see a clock inside my head;
the numbers are a blur."
This symbol, in the notes I read
caused time to be obscured.

"Perhaps that's what we need!"
I said to Larry with delight.
"The years they picked up speed
and so the clinic wasn't right.
The right place, yes indeed.
I bet the clocks were out of sight."
I think the token is the key
and we should bring it back tonight."

As we approached the clinic gate
we could see it was repaired.
Around the fence we'd navigate
and find our way inside of there.
The building now was looking great;
through open windows we both glared.
Although we did not know the date,
we climbed inside despite our fear.

The antenna that we made
had to be left out on the ground.
By the window it would stay
as we made our way around.
The walls were painted pale gray
with several hallways to go down.
Each door led us to a bay
from where we heard a muffled sound.

In every room were seven beds.
In each bed lay a man.
White sheets were placed over their heads.

Leather buckles bound their hands.
Upon each bed digits read
several numbers across a band.
We wondered if they all were dead
with resurrections planned.

Ed was in the first bed
and did not appear as harmed.
Brien was beside him
as was Oscar and was Rom.
Larry saw his himself
and instantly became alarmed.
As his eyes they changed to red,
he blocked the exit with his arm.

I thought for sure he would attack.
Instead he viewed his copied self.
Then he emptied every rack
and he emptied every shelf.
Pouring liquids on his back,
he then set fire to himself.
My vision then turned black
and so I could not save myself.

I awoke to a bright light
and equipment that was beeping.
My wrists were bandaged tight
to keep the blood from my arms seeping.
"Everything will be alright,"
I heard, as I continued sleeping.

It seemed I cut my wrists.
The rest was all just in my mind.
I was relieved to learn of this,
so glad to know that I'd be fine.
I was eventually dismissed.
Amongst my things, what did I find?
Larry's token was on the list.
I guess from now on it is mine.

About the Authors

Amber Bliss (Editor) holds an MFA in Writing Popular Fiction from Seton Hill University and an MLIS from the University of Rhode Island. With a combination of creativity, determination, and a little sorcery, she's managed to combine her passion for writing and tabletop RPGs with her work as a librarian. Amber's days are consumed by stories, whether she's writing them, reading them, or telling them around a table cluttered with dice and character sheets because stories don't only make us werewolves and wizards, they make us human. Her own work can be found in *The Monstrous Feminine* by Scary Dairy Press. You can visit Amber at www.amberbliss.com or find her and her RPG crew's chaotic adventures with DMs After Dark on all the socials and wherever you consume your podcasts.

Sara Deignan (Editor) holds an MLIS from the University of Rhode Island and a BA in English with a Concentration in Writing & Rhetoric from the University of Rhode Island. She has been writing since she could hold a pencil, and before that she dictated her works to her family. She enjoys her work as a librarian, a career that allows her to pursue two of her great passions: being creative and making a good deal of noise. In her free time, Sara enjoys reading spooky stories, spending time with family and friends, and walking her cat Baboo.

Benjamin Fortier grew up in Northern Rhode Island. He enlisted in the Marine Corps Reserve and within ten days of graduating from high school, he was standing on the yellow footprints at Parris Island. In 2006, he served as an infantry team member with 1st Battalion, 25th Marines in Fallujah, Iraq. His latest book, *Phantoms*, was awarded the Robert A. Gannon Award for poetry dealing with Marine Corps life. He is currently serving as the vice president of the 1st Battalion, 25th Marines Association. www.benjaminfortier.com

John Gillard, M.A. "Jesus Christ is my Lord and savior. Everything of value I am, have accomplished, and will accomplish is derived from this fact, including holding a Master's degree in Human Development and Counseling, and an undergraduate degree in Workforce, Education, and Development. Poetry offers rhyme and reason to an often rhythmless and profoundly neurotic world."

Patrick Lachey is following in his father's, grandfather's and great-grandfather's footsteps by seeing the world and serving his country. Patrick is a fourth generation Veteran who served in the USMC and USCG. From jumping out of airplanes and working on large caliber cannons to landing helicopters on ships and chasing drug runners on the open sea, Patrick has had a wonderful career with the military. After leaving active duty, he followed his passion for helping Veterans better their quality of life by helping them navigate the sea of resources through community outreach. His love of movies and comics has led to a creative perspective that started his writing career. Whether it's poetry and short stories or making up tales to tell to his children before bed, the creative passion is always there. Patrick lives in Rhode

Island with his family and can be followed on Instagram at @L4CH3Y

Thomas (Tom) Morrissey (CW3, US Army) is a Veteran, visual/mixed multi-media artist, and writer who has always been sensitive to the exclusion of the many obvious linkages between the arts and (for lack of better words), Veterans. The "military experience," particularly since the Korean/Vietnam eras, has been marginalized at best, and throughout Tom's professional career, he has grown more and more sensitive to this fact, especially as we have now entered the eras of "Post Truth," and "Thank you for your service."

His career in the arts began with his college photography professor instructing him to throw away the few thousand images he returned from the war with. "Guilt," he was told. Throughout his education (PhD, CAGS, MFA, MPA, BFA, AA), his Veteran status was never fully understood, much less beckoned. Decades later, he would learn that many (most) of his "academic heroes" like Peter Voulkos, Don Reitz, and others (yes, he was a ceramic sculpture major), were combat Veterans—a secret never discussed in the years following the fall of Saigon. What might he have done, had anyone mentioned this fact? Fortunately, Tom may still have a few good years in which to flourish. He has more to write.

His professional career has been a multi-directional path. He often says that there are motorboats and sailboats in life. His experience was that of a sailboat; enjoying the various headings tacking in the wind brought him to. Since college, and during his academic career, he has had the honor of returning to Vietnam on several occasions, always alone as with his first visit. He has again left his mark there through a large outdoor marble sculpture installed in Hue (Second International Sculpture Symposium) and by teaching classes in art in Hanoi and Saigon as a Fulbright Scholar. His book, a seventeen-year photo essay, *Between the Lines: Photographs from the National Vietnam Veterans Memorial, Washington DC,* was published in 2000 by Syracuse University Press. Now, Professor Emeritus, he still keeps his hand in teaching, exhibiting, and blowing hot air.

SSgt. Jacob Parkinson was born on an Air Force base in northern California, moved to Texas at age four, and joined the United States Marine Corps at age twenty-one. While serving with India Co 3/5, a boat company, a then Sgt. Parkinson and a fellow squad leader each lost half their squads during the April 8, 2000, MV-22 Osprey crash in Marana, Arizona on the first use infantry deployment of the experimental aircraft. Sgt. Parkinson would go on to serve one combat tour to the Al Anbar Province, Iraq dubbed: The Red Triangle, from 2004 to 2005 as an infantry squad leader, Bravo Co 1/23. At the time, Sgt. Parkinson and his squad would stand defiantly against the cowardice of their platoon commander outside of Fallujah, zero-dark-thirty. That moment sealed the concrete bond formed by 1st squad on that lonely, infamous, November night. SSgt. Parkinson graduated company honorman from bootcamp (#1 out of 500), was meritoriously promoted twice, and is the recipient of several certificates of commendation. He was awarded the Navy Achievement Medal with V for decisive actions taken towards the enemy during combat operations in the Anbar Province. The former Marine is the author of the forthcoming military saga *The Last Letter*, chronicling the writer's time in the Marine Corps. Upon leaving the Marines, SSgt. Parkinson used his military benefits to achieve a bachelor's degree in psychology from the University of Rhode Island in 2020.

Vincent Scirocco is a Rhode Island native. He has an ASET from NEIT and a BSEE from NEU. He has worked for several high-tech electronic and energy companies including BOSE, Hannah Instruments, Teradyne, National Grid, and Eagle-Picher. He has a Lifetime Master Technician Certification and won NEU's TOI Design Challenge by Augmented Reality and drones.

Vincent served in the RIANG from 1987 to 2006, which included an Iraq deployment and a two year recovery period during which he published his collection *Seasons Of Reasons* and created a Veterans Awareness Monument that was dedicated to the City of Woonsocket, RI in 2005.

He has spent the last two decades volunteering with various Veterans' organizations and served as Veterans of Foreign Wars Dept. of RI Commander from 2010 to 2011. More recently, Vincent graduated from the Providence Clemente Veterans Initiative (PCVI). He enjoys sharing poetry, believes his writing skills are a result of his struggles, and hopes to inspire others.

Dennis Zambrotta is a USN Veteran who has served actively as an Operations Specialist and as a Department of the Navy civilian attached to the Naval War College. He retired in 2019 after over forty years of service. He has been an avid striped bass surfcaster for the past fifty years and has pursued his quarry from Montauk to Cape Cod and many points in between. He has authored two books: *Surfcasting Around the Block* which is widely considered the definitive guide to surfcasting Block Island, and *Surfcasting Around the Block II*, which covers Block and Aquidneck Islands. He has also written numerous articles for *The Fisherman Magazine*, *On the Water*, and *Surfcasters Journal*.

Glossary

AC: Aircraft Commander

AWOL: Absent Without Leave

Basic: Basic training

Bivouacked: To provide temporary quarters for

Boonie Cap: A soft hat worn by combat infantrymen in the field

C&C: Command and Control

CA: Combat Assault

Cadet: Warrant Officer Candidate

Cammies: The standard uniform Marines wear in garrison, during training, and while deployed overseas

Checkride: A practical flight test necessary to receive pilot certification

Chip Detector: Indicator light on an instrument panel used to detect metal chips, shavings, or particles present in aircraft engine and transmission lubrication systems

CO: Commanding Officer

Cobras: Attack Helicopters

DEROS: Date Estimated Return from Overseas

Deuce and a Half: M35 series 2½-ton 6×6 cargo truck

DFC: Distinguished Flying Cross

Donut Dollies: Women who volunteered in Vietnam with the American Red Cross

Fire Support Base: A temporary facility that provides artillery support to the infantry

Flak: A form of body armor designed to provide protection from case fragments high explosive weaponry

Full Birds: Full Colonels

Gook: Offensive and derogatory slang term for Asian and Vietnamese people

Ground Pounders: A slang term for infantry soldiers

Grunt: A slang term for infantry soldiers

Hootch: A hut or simple dwelling, either military or civilian

Huey: Bell UH-1 Iroquois helicopter

IED: An improvised explosive device

IP: Instructor Pilot

KIA: Killed In Action

Klick: kilometer

Latrine: Bathroom

LRRP: long-range reconnaissance patrol

M-1 Abrams: A third-generation American main battle tank

MACV: Military Assistance Command, Vietnam (Same as MACVSOG)

MACVSOG: Military Assistance Command, Vietnam-Studies and Observations Group

MIA: Missing In Action

MOS: Military Occupational Specialty

MVP: Million Veteran Program

NVA: North Vietnamese Army

NVGs: Night Vision Goggles

O-Club: Officers' Club

Otters: An amphibious cargo transport

PBR: River patrol boat

Peter-pilot: Co-pilot

POL: Abbreviation for petroleum, oil, and lubricants

REMF: Rear Echelon Mother Fucker, slang for someone far from the front lines, intended as insult

Replacement Battalion: A unit of reserves for entering or leaving Vietnam

Revetment Area: An aircraft parking area

SDS: Students for a Democratic Society

SEAL: Navy Sea, Air, and Land Teams, component of the Naval Special Warfare Command

Tet: Vietnamese Lunar New Year

Tet Offensive: A major escalation in the Vietnam War

TOC: Tactical Operations Center

USO: The United Service Organization provided entertainment to the troops, and was intended to raise morale

Vietnamization: U.S. policy initiated by President Richard Nixon late in the war to turn over the fighting to the South Vietnamese Army during the phased withdrawal of American troops

VIPs in 58s: Flying high ranking officers in smaller Bell OH-58 Kiowa observation helicopters

VNAF: Vietnam Air Force

WJC: Worcester Junior College

XO: Executive officer; the second in command of a military unit